WINTER KILL

45

z J

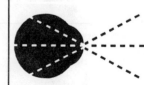

This Large Print Book carries the
Seal of Approval of N.A.V.H.

WINTER KILL

FRANK RODERUS

WHEELER PUBLISHING
An imprint of Thomson Gale, a part of The Thomson Corporation

THOMSON

GALE

Detroit • New York • San Francisco • New Haven, Conn. • Waterville, Maine • London

Copyright © 2001 by Frank Roderus.

Thomson Gale is part of The Thomson Corporation.

Thomson and Star Logo and Wheeler are trademarks and Gale is a registered trademark used herein under license.

Wheeler Publishing Large Print Western.

The text of this Large Print edition is unabridged.

Other aspects of the book may vary from the original edition.

Set in 16 pt. Plantin.

LIBRARY OF CONGRESS CATALOGING-IN-PUBLICATION DATA

Roderus, Frank, 1942–
    Winter kill / by Frank Roderus.
        p. cm. — (Wheeler Publishing large print western)
    ISBN 1-59722-383-2 (alk. paper)
    1. Cattle stealing — Fiction. 2. Large type books. I. Title.
    PS3568.O346W56 2006

2006029345

U.S. Softcover:
ISBN 13: 978-1-59722-383-6
ISBN 10: 1-59722-383-2

Published in 2006 by arrangement with Frank Roderus.

Printed in the United States of America on permanent paper
10 9 8 7 6 5 4 3 2 1

WINTER KILL

1

The old witch's nerve broke and she came busting out of the thicket in an explosion of snapping twigs and trampled leaves, her calf about half a jump behind her and just as spooky as she was.

The horse didn't have to be told what needed doing. It was already digging and scrambling after her and not looking for any easy route to get there.

Jug tried to make himself small — not all that difficult a thing to do, considering — by laying flat over the brown horse's neck and throwing an elbow in front of his face to keep all those wickedly brittle branches from poking him in the eyes.

The cow and calf tore off down the mountainside, Jug and the brown larruping behind. Jug kneed the horse right just a little, taking the high side of things on the slope to make sure the cow angled downhill. The cow didn't know it, but down was where he wanted her to go.

Their commotion dislodged a cascade of gravel and small chunks, and they probably weren't making any more noise than six brass bands as they barged into, over, through, and around whatever came in their way. The cow was huffing and the calf bawling and the both of them squirting yellow streams out from under their tails.

The brown tucked its forelegs tight up to its chest and went sailing over the top of a deadfall pine tree that was laying too dang high for any horse to clear and if they'd smashed into it the impact would've killed the both of them, but the fool horse didn't know it couldn't make that jump and cleared the bark of the tree trunk by half a foot.

Jug was so impressed that he glanced backward for half a second.

The spooky old cow, teaching her baby her own cantankerous ways, tried to double back on them, but the brown was up to that trick and spun as fast as a man turning to look when a gust of spring wind lifts a lady's hem.

They were clearing the worst of the timber and getting down toward the steep stuff, so Jug quit acting like a tick on the brown's neck and came upright a little.

It was probably a good thing he did that for the cow reversed herself again, and the brown hits its hocks in a butt-down slide to come back with her.

The bad thing was that neither horse nor man saw the patch where a flow of melt from a pocket of crusted old snow had turned the ground into slick and slippery goo underneath a thin layer of gravel.

The brown's hind legs went out from under it quick as a bawdy girl's wink.

Jug didn't have time to fret about it.

He felt the brown's hindquarters slide and more heard than felt it when he and the horse both hit the ground — hard — and went skidding down the slope in a wobbly spin like a top that's just about come to a stop.

Jug's left leg was caught underneath the brown and his right foot was still in the stirrup. He knew he was getting scraped up something awful, but between the old-fashioned rawhide leggings that he still favored and the protection of a stout coat it shouldn't be too awful bad.

Dang horse was flailing its legs and whipping its neck, trying to get back upright while it was still sliding down the hillside. Jug wished it would lay still and ride this out because every time it tried to throw itself its weight pressed full onto Jug's leg and that wasn't fun.

About then they reached the bottom. Slid smack off a little rock ledge and dropped two, three feet onto the broken rock and washed-down junk in the small end of that gully.

Jug felt the drop, then the side of his head smacked into something with a sound like a rotten watermelon being dropped onto hard ground.

He remembered hearing that.

Didn't remember another dang thing after.

2

Fuzz. That's what he could see. Nothing but fuzz in different colors. Blue. That was sky, prob'ly. Brown. Could be most anything. Red. That was . . . red? He blinked and shook his head, trying to clear some of the fuzz away.

Big mistake. Shouldn't shake his fool head like that. It hurt. God, it hurt. Like to made him sick to his stomach it hurt so bad.

But the shaking, the blinking, something helped. He blinked several more times and was able to make out that the red was the segundo's rumpled old red bandanna hanging at his throat like it always did and the brown was his hat. Jesse was leaning over him. Saying something that Jug couldn't make out.

Jug dang near shook his head again to try to clear it, but he remembered in time and didn't make that mistake a second time. He settled for blinking some more and shoot-

11

ing his jaw in an effort to clear his ears. He heard somebody groan and after a moment realized it'd been him that made the sound. Embarrassing, that was.

"You all right, you old fart?" Jesse was asking him.

"Hell, yes. I'm fine."

"You're a damn liar, too," the segundo accused.

Jug managed a grin. "Watch your mouth, boy, lest I take you out behind the woodshed." He prob'ly wasn't any more than six or seven years older than Jesse. But it felt like more. By God, it did. He felt a little better, though, for being able to snap back like that. He struggled, trying to lever himself upright. If he could just get onto his own hind legs he'd be all right. He was sure of it.

"Lay still, old man."

"What's the matter? Am I busted up or something?" He tried to keep the concern out of his voice.

"No, dammit, you didn't bust nothing. Lucky for you it was your head that got whacked an' it was harder than whatever you hit." Jesse grinned. "Probably hit a damn rock an' broke it. If you want I'll have the boys scout around and see can they find the pieces so's you can have a souvenir."

Jug chuckled a bit. The tiny movement made his head hurt again. Maybe Jesse was right. Maybe he should lay still for another minute or two.

"You mashed your leg some, but we looked it over. Don't think you broke it." Jesse's grin returned. "You're gonna be purple for a spell though, I bet. If you go an' die on us I reckon we'll skin you an' tack the hide up on the bunkhouse wall. It'd be right colorful."

"You can have the leg, damn you, but you know what I want done with the rest of my hide if it comes t' that," Jug told him.

Jesse laughed. "Course I do. You've told it often enough. Have your scrawny hide tanned an' sewed into the seat of a pretty lady's saddle."

"Exactly," Jug said. "That way I can spend eternity between the two things I like the best, a good horse an'. . . . well . . . the other." He laughed. That hurt him, but it was worth it. He could see and hear much better now. Finding out his leg wasn't broke helped. As for his head, well, a man has to take some knocks now and again. Either that or go to store clerking for his living, and Jug wasn't ready to lower himself to that quite yet.

"Somebody pick up that miserable ol'

bitch and her calf?" he asked.

"Sure. We seen you come down that hill. Pretty good chase while it lasted. You know what's funny? That old hillside outlaw got herself down into the bottom of that draw and seen the rest of the gather. Damned if she didn't walk into the bunch just as sweet-tempered as an old milk cow and her calf alongside of her."

"How 'bout the horse?"

Jesse paused half a second, which was enough to tell Jug what he wanted to know. "Busted the left fore all to splinters, Jug. I'm sorry. I know you favored that un."

"Ayuh. Good horse. I'm sorry I went an' lost him. My fault though, not his. I should've been watching closer."

Jesse nodded. "Billy the kid got your gear off him. It's in the possum belly under the cook wagon."

"All right."

"When you feel up to getting around some you can ride with Coosie."

"I'm not dead, dammit, and you said yourself nothing's busted. I can still ride."

"Course you could still ride, you miser-able old son of a bitch. Except that we don't have no spare horse to put you on."

"Oh."

"Just lay here a bit more an' get to feeling

better. When we're ready to move over t' work the next drainage we'll haul you down to the wagon an' load your skinny ass in with the flour an' beans."

"You will if I don't decide t' whup you and take that horse away from you," Jug declared.

Jesse laughed. "You'll be all right, Jug. Lay still now an' contemplate the errors of your ways. I got work t' do."

"Yeah, go off an' leave me if you like."

"You want I should set beside you an' hold your hand?"

"No, but you could fetch that Lucy girl up here t' do it for you."

Jesse rolled his eyes and laughed again. "If I could do that, Jug, I surely would. Now lay still an' get your sense back . . . what little you had t' begin with. And don't be in no hurry about it. We'll be here for a little while yet till the boys working the south slope bring theirs down to the gather. No hurry for you to move around, an' the truth is that you're still pretty pale underneath that leather you wear for skin an' your speech is kinda slurry an' slow. You bonked yourself pretty good, Jug. Damn if you didn't."

"All right then. Go on an' get to the things that need doing. I'm fine here."

Jesse stood and headed down the draw toward where Jug could hear the grunt and shuffle of cattle pacing aimlessly about and the creak and jangle of saddles as the younger hands held them in a bunch.

Jug lay back — somebody'd stuffed his hat under his head to act as a pillow, and he appreciated that — and tried to ignore the pounding in his head and the deeper pain that filled his whole left side from the ribs down.

There were days when he came real near to thinking he was getting too damned old for this business. Of course, he was wrong when he thought that. But it did sneak into his mind now and again, and this was turning out to be one of those days. It surely was.

3

Jug scowled and scanned the ground ahead for rocks. Oh Lordy, he was coming to hate rocks. Rocks and ruts and bumps in the way, anything that made the wagon jolt and rattle. The dang thing had no more spring to it than a pine-slat bed, and every pebble they drove over hurt like hell.

No point in saying anything to Coosie about it, of course. The man couldn't avoid every bump on the ground and anyway it was already clear that he was doing his best to make it a smooth ride. It was just that they were — what? — twenty, thirty miles from what might pass for a road and this wasn't country that would coddle a man.

The left front wheel rose high onto a slab of gray stone and the seat tilted; Jug braced himself. When the wheel jounced down again the shock of it sent a rip of fresh pain all through Jug's left side and he gritted his teeth to keep from making a noise over it.

The least he could do was act like a damn man about this now that he'd gone and done it.

Coosie — Jug had no idea what the man's right name was but it seemed like all ranch cooks come to be called Coosie, whatever name they might've started out with — reached behind his seat and brought out a plug of tobacco. He offered it first to Jug, who declined the generosity — the plug had a thin coat of what looked like mule hair all over it and God knew where it'd been rattling around for the last dozen or so years to get in such a condition — then grunted and bit off a chew for himself.

"Hang on," Coosie said, dropping the plug onto the floor of the driving box and grabbing hold of his lines with both hands while he slowed the mules and guided them into a tippy-toe descent through a washed out slash in the ground.

The wagon lurched and swayed and tipped so far over to one side that it almost scared Jug half to death from thinking the whole thing was going to topple over and wreck him for the second time in one day. Jug wasn't damn used to riding on wheels and didn't like it. Not a lick, he didn't.

Coosie, on the other hand, scarcely seemed to notice.

"Are you aware," Jug said casually so as to hide his concern, "that you've got more hair coming out of your ears than I got on my head?"

Coosie snorted. He also kept his attention on the mules as he set them into a lurching, heart-stopping rush up the other side of the shallow, sharp-walled cut and onto firm ground again.

"Got you a pretty good crop of nose hair, too," Jug observed. "I hear tell there's a pretty good cash market for that. If you want I can mow an' bale it for you when we get back t' the bunkhouse."

"Will you shut the hell up, old man? I'm trying to think here an' you're distracting me."

"What're you thinking about, Coosie?"

"Trying to figure out what to sneak into the soup tonight," he said in a steady, thoughtful tone. "Got to choose, you see. Betwixt lizard livers and buzzard guts. It's a quandary, I tell you. Been vexing me this whole day long."

"Always been fond of liver myself, if that helps any."

"I'll keep that in mind, thank you." Then he added, "Uh-oh," and another terse, "Hang on," as they came to yet another washout left from the spring melt.

19

Jug grabbed hold of the seat with both white-knuckled hands and did what he was told. Lordy, he was glad Coosie was responsible for the driving and not him. These dang wagons just naturally scared the bejabbers out of a man.

4

"You're looking fit," Jesse observed.

"As a fiddle," Jug agreed cheerfully.

"Feeling up to getting back t' work, are you?"

"Hell yes. A man gets tired just laying around reading the labels on cans. Wouldn't be so bad, I expect, except that damn Coosie has terrible taste in canned goods. But then he has to pick out the ones with pictures on 'em so's he'll know what's inside."

Coosie was standing about five feet away and was certain to hear every word. Of course, if he hadn't been there would've been no point in throwing the rowels to him.

"Good," Jesse said. "I kinda thought you'd feel that way about it. But you shouldn't push yourself in too big a hurry."

"I'm fine," Jug assured the lanky segundo. "I can do whatever's needed." He said it with as straight a pitch as ever he knew how, but the truth was that the thought of shaking around on top of a rough-and-ready circle horse came awfully close to unnerving him. It had been — what? — three days? And he was still red and purple all over his left side. Worse, it still hurt so bad he couldn't sleep at night and 'most any sort of movement brought cold sweat popping out all over his body from the pain shooting through. Just lying down at night was a study in applied agony. And having to stand up again in the morning after a night lying on the cold hard ground was worse yet.

The outfit wasn't paying him to lay around and sop biscuits in cold coffee though, so if Jesse needed him to act like a hand again, well, that's what he'd have to do. There'd be time enough for healing come next winter.

He stood up from the keg where he'd been resting and hoped he was able to keep from showing what it cost him to get up onto his own hind legs.

"Didn't figure you'd feel up to dancing around inside the remuda," Jesse said, "so I told Billy he should dab a loop onto whatever of your string was handy."

"That's thoughtful of you."

A minute or so later here came Billy the kid all right. Damned idiot boy was leading the hardest-headed, most cantankerous son of a bitch in Jug's whole string. The horse was about as good a wide-circle horse as a man could want. It was one of those spotted-ass things with the funny-looking pale eyes and a spotted white blanket over its butt. Jug had heard tell that they were Indian bred and maybe they were. He didn't know about that. What he did know for certain sure was that there wasn't a brain between the stupid creature's ears. Dumbest damned horse he'd ever been around and spooky as a ha'nt on Halloween. It'd booger at anything. And if there wasn't anything around to scare it, well, it'd invent something to be scared of.

The Indian horse was also, however, one of the toughest animals Jug ever saddled. He doubted it'd be possible to wear the ugly thing down even if you tried to do it deliberate.

None of those things was what worried him now though. The thought that made his skin crawl at the sight of Billy coming with the spotted horse was the fact that it had a ride that'd break a man's teeth. And that was when it was walking. Its trot would rattle a man's head until little bitty pieces of broken brain dribbled out his ears if he wasn't careful to keep his head perfectly level.

No, sir, it wasn't with any pleasure that he watched Billy lead the danged Indian horse near.

"This one be all right, Mr. Jug?" Billy asked.

"Sure, kid. It's the one I would've chose my own self." Like hell. It was not only the dumbest horse in his bunch it was far and away the tallest, too, and would be the hardest to get onto.

"Mr. Jesse told me I should try to get you the blue roan, but he kept ducking out from under my throw. I guess I need to get some more roping lessons off you, huh?"

"You did fine, boy. Now where'd I put my saddle?"

"Let me do it for you, Mr. Jug," Billy offered so nicely that Jug didn't have the heart to tell him no, never mind, that it saved him the hurting of going after his gear, which was still laying in the possum belly underneath the grub wagon.

"You don't have to work today if you don't want," Jesse offered while Billy got Jug's saddle and strapped it onto the spotted horse.

"Aw, I'm fine."

"All right. Have at 'er."

And that damned Jesse stood there saying not a word while Jug embarrassed hell out of himself trying to do as simple a dang thing as step onto his own saddle.

Try as he might — and try he surely did — he couldn't bend that left leg nor lift it high enough to get his foot into the stirrup.

Embarrassing? It was worse than mere embarrassment. It was purely mortifying is what it was.

"Jug," Jesse said when Jug finally accepted his limitation and went around to crawl on from the right side instead.

"What!" Jug snapped back at him, not even caring that it came out as peevish and waspy as he felt by now.

"I didn't think you'd tell me the truth about how bad it is," Jesse accused. "Figured you'd have to show yourself as well as me. Fact is, you need to rest up and get that leg to being useful. T' say nothing about the ribs I expect you went an' broke. You did bust you some ribs, didn't you?"

"Not many," Jug swore.

"I'm sending you down t' the home place. We're moving camp tomorrow, and Coosie's gonna go down an' reprovision. I want you to go down with him. Tell the foreman what happened. An' before you go to wondering, there won't be anybody using any of your string till you get back. You hear me?"

Jug wanted to protest and show the damn segundo that he could still do a day's work.

Except, well, except he wasn't so almighty sure that he could.

Right now, that is.

Maybe it would be better if he got himself healed up a little before he went to chasing cows again. Maybe. "Whatever you say, Jesse," he said, meek as meek could be.

5

"What are you doing down here, old man? You aren't intending to draw your pay, are you?"

"And deprive the outfit of the best hand you got? Not no way I'd do that, Eli. But the other boys was getting kinda jealous, what with me bringing in all the beef and them not having much of anything to do once I got done with my gather. You know how it is."

"Yes, I do know and that's why I'm asking for the truth," the foreman responded. He'd been crossing the ranch yard toward the chow hall when Jug stepped out of the bunkhouse and practically bumped into him.

"Yeah, well, maybe I had a little bit of a wreck," Jug said. "Cost the outfit that brown horse. You can dock my pay if you like."

"I'm not gonna dock your pay for a damn horse. Are you all right?"

"Will be but, well, maybe I need some mending. Jesse said I should come down and lay around a spell."

"All right then. You'll have to wrestle your own grub though. It'll just be you and me and you don't want any of my cooking. That'd set back your healing processes. Hell, it makes me sick eating it myself."

Eli eyed him for a second or two, and Jug could read plain as plain in the foreman's expression what he was thinking. He stopped short of asking it though, asking would Jug be willing to cook for the both of them. That would have been the next thing to stating outright that Jug was due for retirement from horseback work. Would have been almost, not quite, as bad as if Jesse or Eli lent some other hand a horse out of Jug's string or asked the old cowboy to get down off his saddle and dig holes for fenceposts. Any of those would add up to being a suggestion that Jug either swallow his pride or draw his time. To which Jug would've had to ask for his riding-on pay. Bum leg and busted ribs or no, he was still a hand and expected to stay one just as far ahead as he could see.

"I can boil water an' burn bacon, I reckon," Jug said, then added, "for the both of us," there being a whopping big difference between Eli telling him to cook and Jug himself making the offer.

"I expect we'll make out all right then." Eli took his hat off and scratched his head some. The man had hair as red as any beet that's ever been grown and a full head of it, unlike some people. Jug didn't know how old Eli Poole was, but would've guessed it at barely into his thirties. And already foreman of as fine an outfit there was anyplace in the Bear Creek drainage. He was a comer, Eli was. Everybody said that. And he knew cows and cowboys. Everybody said that, too. He'd grown up in New Mexico, cowboyed in Arizona for a spell, then got smart and came north onto the big grass country of Wyoming and Montana. Now here he was, boss of the M Bar C. He was a comer all right. Ambitious and a real go-getter. Everybody said that.

Jug didn't like the son of a bitch. Didn't know why. Just didn't cotton to him much. Maybe it was all that damned red hair, Jug himself being the next best thing to bald. Or the tidy little mustache that lay curled over the top of his upper lip like a rat's tail lying snug over a rat ass. Something. Jug couldn't put a finger to it.

The good thing, of course, was that you don't have to like a man to work for him.

29

Thank goodness.

And Eli did know his business. Jug had to give him that.

And if Jug wished the job had gone to Jesse Canfield when the owners had to find a replacement for Clay Bannerman, rest his soul, well, that wasn't any business of an ordinary working hand like Jug. Ranch management and high finance and all that stuff, that was beyond Jug's ken and even farther from his interest.

All Jug wanted was to have a decent string of horses and use them to ride free like a man ought to. Give the outfit an honest day of work and have a good ol' time once in a while when the town lights dazzled and the powdered ladies earned their pay . . . or his, which amounted to the same thing.

Anyway, what in hell was he doing standing around thinking dumb thoughts like that when there was yet work to be done? He might not be up for much but there ought to be something he could do to help Coosie get ready to pull out and head back to the gather come tomorrow daybreak.

Coosie would take care of his own mules — woe to anyone but him who laid a finger on any of those pampered long-ears — but there was a wagon to load and likely some other chores that needed doing, and Jug wasn't useless yet, by jingo.

He told the foreman g'day and limped off toward the chow hall.

6

Jug hung the iron bar back on the hook where it belonged. His hand tingled slightly from the reverberations of the triangle that was used to call the hands to meals.

Eli was scowling when he approached. "You don't have to ring it so damn much. I'm not deaf."

Jug shrugged. His habit was to clang the iron and keep on clanging it until the foreman came out onto the porch. It wasn't that Jug worried that Eli hadn't heard. He just plain liked to clang the triangle. "Whatever you say," he said, knowing full well that he would conveniently forget that promise by lunchtime.

"Breakfast ready?" Eli asked.

"Ayuh." It was a stupid question. Why else would he have rung the dinner bell if it hadn't been? But then Poole's question wasn't really a question, more like a polite way of making conversation without having to say anything.

They went inside to a table intended to seat as many as a dozen and a half men at a time. The place seemed almost empty with just the two of them there.

Jug had the meal all cooked and laid ready. Coffee, of course. Chunks of bacon. About a half gallon of bacon gravy — dang stuff just kept growing once he started trying to add a little of this or a bit of that in his attempts to get it right — and some yellow and brown lumps that were as close as he could come to making biscuits. It was just a good thing that he wasn't ready to retire to ranch cooking yet for any crew he cooked for would surely draw their time and move on after a couple days of eating at his table.

The fact that Eli had kept coming back for three days now didn't speak to Jug's abilities so much as it illuminated the foreman's lack of culinary skill. Eli's cooking must be *really* awful.

Each of them grabbed a heavy crockery plate and mug off the sideboard and carried them to the table, Eli taking his rightful place at the head and Jug sitting beside him. Usually Jug preferred to stay down at the foot end where the segundo's regular place was, but with only him and Eli eating that

33

would've been rude.

"Got anything planned today?" Eli asked.

"You're the foreman. You tell me."

"You feeling up to doing some riding?"

"You bet." And it was, in fact, the truth. He wasn't feeling good but he was a far sight better now than he'd been when Coosie carried him down in that infernal wagon. He was able to bend his left leg now. A little. It hurt when he did it, of course, but at least he could do it. And he'd torn an old blanket into strips and used that to bind his chest to keep the broken ribs from hurting quite so bad as they had been.

The ribs would take a couple months to really heal. He knew that. Lord knew he'd busted ribs often enough in years past to know what to expect. But with tight binding the pain was bearable.

"Good. I have some errands to run, so I'd like you to ride down to Bonner for me."

"I can do that." Errands, the man said. Jug knew what sort of "errand" Eli would be about. There wasn't but one place in thirty, forty miles where a man might go to perform a legitimate errand and that was Bonner. Apart from a couple hog ranches where a man could get liquored up or buy some time with a cheap whore, Bonner was the only place a man could go for shopping or mail or whatever.

What the foreman had in mind was something else entire. Eli had himself a lady friend. A married lady friend. The whole crew knew it. Jug didn't know if Eli was aware of that, but it was true. Time to time, Eli would go riding off to "check the grass" or "look at calves" or some such flimsy excuse.

Funny thing was that Eli's errands always coincided with Abe Goodrun being off on some errand of his own. Whatever took Abe away from home and his young wife meant it was time for Eli to go off on an errand, too.

Jug didn't know how Miz Goodrun let Eli know that Abe would be away, but she managed it somehow and Eli would go off for the day or sometimes for several days in a row if poor Abe was away shipping beef or something.

It was a crying shame about Abe but none of Jug's nevermind. "What d'you have in mind for me to do in the big city?" Jug asked, as if he hadn't a clue about what Eli was really up to.

7

The trip to Bonner wasn't so awful bad except for taking twice as long as usual. Jug saddled the outfit's Lady Horse, the slow and settled creature that hadn't fire enough to be a man's proper mount yet was sound and strong and could be counted on to not booger nor cause trouble if a visitor — one of the investors, say, or, worst of all, an investor's wife — wanted to go for a pleasure ride.

You never knew what some silly dang investor might do. Jug saw one once insist on having fresh cream for his lady's tea. Wanted somebody to milk a cow for him and couldn't understand why they didn't keep fresh milk in the spring house since there were so many cows all over the dang place. Would've been different if he wanted to milk the cow himself. That woulda been kind of fun to watch. Instead he wanted it done for him and the cream brought to him.

They'd gotten together, Clay — he'd still been foreman then — and Jesse and a couple of the other hands, just about all of whom had moved along by now, and talked it over. It was either put on one helluva rodeo, for which they might as well advertise and sell tickets, or lie to the man. So, of course, they lied to the man. Poured regular evaporated milk into a crockery mug, smudged the rim of the cup so as to look like it'd been hard used, and presented it for the sweet young thing's tea. She never knew the difference. Wasn't the investor's wife neither as Jug learned a couple years after when that same investor and three others came out on one of their infrequent inspections. Which usually was for the purpose of shooting critters and carousing except this time the real wives came along, too.

Funny, but the inspection trips weren't so popular after that.

Anyhow the outfit still kept a few Lady Horses around just in case one of the investors took a notion to be wild and woolly. So Jug saddled this one and crawled on from the off side, that left leg not yet so much better that using it to mount a horse was a good idea.

Clamping down hard with his legs or even

using his knees properly would've been plenty uncomfortable but a Lady Horse could be ridden by a sack of potatoes and not cause trouble, so all Jug had to do was sit up on top of the thing and aim it where he wanted to go.

Which in this case was Bonner, Wyoming. The State of, if you please, Wyoming having been admitted to the Union as a regular state just a couple years back. Jug felt a certain amount of pride over that, albeit a pride that was mixed in with some other feelings, too. When he'd first come up here with a trail herd of stockers, about the only law in Wyoming Territory was what a man knew to be right or wrong. Now they wanted to put it all down on paper and hire lawyers to decide right from wrong. Jug wasn't entirely sure that was an improvement.

Still, they were a state now and that was progress.

He took the Lady Horse down the road at a slow and steady gait that would've been embarrassing if there been anybody to see it, and by the middle of the afternoon he could see what passed for the big city around here. Normally he would've made it in time for lunch but not this time down.

That was all right. He wasn't coming in for any purpose that would get a man's blood to bubbling, and if it got too late going back that evening he could just close his eyes and catch a little nap while the horse did the work. Which, come to think of it, was a decided advantage a Lady Horse can have over a properly lively cayuse.

He thought about seeing if a jab of the spurs would perk up this horse for his entrance to town, then thought better of that notion. Taunt fate so deliberately as that and a man never knows what result he might end up with. So he made the safe and sensible choice and plodded dogged and steady the last couple miles into Bonner.

8

Bonner was a nice enough place. It'd gotten started in a copse of cottonwood trees alongside Hayden Creek, which ran between the runty little Camus Range of low mountains to the east and the much taller and prouder Sheephorn Range that lay off to the west of Bonner and Hayden Creek.

The M Bar C graze took up most of the Bear Creek drainage and lay snug beneath the east slopes of the Sheephorns, Bear Creek being one of half a dozen or so small and sometimes seasonal watercourses that fed into Hayden.

It was fine country, sage flats and rabbitbrush down low, bunchgrasses on the foothills, and a good growth of summer forage up high in the Sheephorns. Spring and fall the outfit's cows grazed the foothills. They summered high. And winters they were kept down on the flats where their diet was supplemented with hay cut by long, sweaty caravans of draft horses, mowers, rakes, and such-like that traveled south to north each year during the haying season, hiring on to do the jobs that individual outfits would've had difficulty managing on their own.

This was good country, Jug thought, and a man could live a good life in it. He'd been here now . . . he had to think on it some . . . two hairs and a whoop-de-doo longer than twenty years. He'd come up out of Texas. Started out tending the remuda for one of old Mr. Sam Silas's early trail herds. Mr. Sam was dead now, Jug heard, but he'd been a good man.

Later Jug made four more trips up the trails to Kansas as a hand. Went from breathing dust in the drag to riding proud on flank and finally rode point for Wilse Peterman on a mean and miserable trip to Ellsworth.

Those had been some years.

He'd trailed cattle across the Pecos into New Mexico and got all the way to Arizona once, then hired on with that crazy SOB Billy Button, who would buy up scrawny heifers in Texas and deliver fat stock cows in Kansas and Nebraska and Dakota, Colorado and Wyoming and all the way to Montana. Billy had a way with cows. Jug sometimes thought the man could put tallow onto a beef's ribs just by looking at the critter and wishing for it to gain. He was always able to buy cheap and sell dear, and that made him a rich man before he was done. Then the tuberculosis took Billy down and despite the fancy tent treatments he got down in Colorado there wasn't anything Billy could do to put meat back onto his own poor ribs. Jug hadn't heard anything from or about Billy in six or eight years. Prob'ly he'd died, too. A heap of Jug's friends had.

It was a fine life those old boys had lived though and a fine one they taught to Jug. He had no regrets and he was sure none of the others from those days did either.

As for now, well, he was plenty content with this country and with the M Bar C.

He walked the Lady Horse into the business district of Bonner and around a corner to one of the alleys so he could dismount without anybody seeing him get off on the wrong side of the dang horse, then went back out into the main street and gave the animal water at the public trough outside Town Hall. That done, he tied the horse to a convenient rail and loosed the cinches on his old rimfire rig, both of them — he still had the Texas habit of preferring two cinches even though he'd long since given up tie-fast roping and had learned to dally.

He patted the left side pocket of his vest to make sure he could still feel the wad of paper Eli Poole gave him that morning, then ambled off toward Bricker's Hardware to place the first of several orders for goods that the outfit was needing.

9

Just hand these papers to the people I tell you. That's what Eli told him to do. Sometimes Jug had the impression that Eli didn't think any of the working hands could read or something. And hell, a few of them couldn't. But most of the boys could read and some of them did. Sometimes the foreman acted like he was the only man in the outfit who had a lick of intelligence or common sense. Come to think of it, maybe that was why Jug didn't like the man. Had something to do with it anyhow.

Handing in the lists was what he'd been told to do though, so that's what he did. Just found each of the merchants named and forked over the shopping lists one by one.

At the hardware they needed bar iron for making horseshoes. Keg of Horseshoe nails. Bales of new rope. The usual stuff.

From Simon down at the grocery and

general mercantile there was a whopping big order for flour, sugar, rice, and coffee. Beans, onions, and potatoes. Everything by the barrel or the hundredweight sack. Tins of milk and tomatoes and peaches by the case. Vinegar and honey by the demikeg. When he saw that, Jug wondered aloud if the foreman intended making some experiments about how to catch flies. That got a dutiful chuckle out of Simon, who no doubt had heard it a couple hundred times before.

There were also a couple items Jug didn't recognize. Those referred to catalogs by page and item number and could have been anything. Jug didn't bother to ask Simon what they were. An outfit the size of the M Bar C — not that it was the biggest he'd ever come across but it was maybe the best — needed a fearsome amount of goods to keep it going.

"I can have this ready for you by morning if you like, Jug."

"No, Eli said he'll send a wagon and a couple youngsters with strong backs in maybe three weeks or so when the outfit comes down outa the foothills. Thought you might need time to order in some of the things."

"Just the hat. The food items I've plenty of, especially at this time of year when everyone is buying heavy for the spring work."

"All right, thanks."

He refrained from asking what hat Simon meant. Had to be one of the catalog items, of course. Jug couldn't hardly imagine a man buying himself a new hat out of a catalog where he couldn't try it on first. But it wasn't any of his business so he kept his jaw shut on the subject.

From the grocery Jug walked down to Tom Hall's saddlery to hand in an order for leather strapping and thread and harness needles. He couldn't help but stop there for a bit to run his hand over the seat of Tom's show-off display saddle set on a wooden stand by the front door so you had to pass by it whenever you came or went.

"That one is yours if you want it, Jug."

Lordy, but that was one fine-looking piece of workmanship. Fully tooled skirts all covered with swirls and oak leaves and acorns. Ivory-colored leather insets at the skirt corners with roping scenes on them. Bits of German silver set here and there. Not too much though. There was nothing gaudy about this saddle.

"I got to tell you true, Tom, this is as pretty a thing as ever I've seen."

"Thank you, Jug. I take that as a high

compliment."

"Which is just how I meant it, Tom."

"If you want it, Jug, I'd make you a price on it. Wouldn't have to pay me now. Ride it home today if you like. You know I'd take your handshake on the deal."

He shook his head. Wasn't even tempted. "Debt is for rich men and fools, Tom." He grinned. "I know I'm not the one an' hope I'm not the other neither. But I thank you for the offer."

"If you change your mind, Jug, that offer will stand. Any time you want that thing, you don't even have to say anything. Just pick it up an' walk out with it. It'll be yours."

"No, I reckon some things aren't meant for poor boys. But I surely do admire this piece. You do fine work." Jug looked at him and laughed. "For a city boy." Tom came off a farm someplace back east in Iowa or one of those places like that. God knew how he wound up here in Bonner but a city boy he was most definitely not.

"What can I do you for?" Tom asked, and they got down to business with Eli's list.

10

Jug's last stop was at the post office window. It wasn't a separate post office building like they had in cities, but John Cade who ran the Bonner Haberdashery and was chairman of the county Republican committee had separated the whole back of his place off and put the post office in there.

Of course, it was only good business for him to put it all the way in the back so a man had to walk past the shelves of ready-to-wear shirts and suits and hats and things in order to get to the mail window. And it was just as good sense for John to cut a doorway through to the side leading into his wife's ladies' wear shop next door, that being to make it nice and easy for women to shop while they happened by to look for mail or get a stamp. John was no fool, for most everybody came to the post office from time to time and they all had to come into his store to do it.

"Anything for the M Bar C crowd?" Jug asked when John got around to opening the window for him. John had been busy waiting on Doug Hawkins when Jug first walked in and the storekeeper wasn't likely to walk away from a five-dollar clothing sale in order to sell a three-cent stamp or hand out free mail for nothing, especially when the three cents would go to the government and not into John's own pocket.

"Oh, I expect I should. Let me see here." John turned away and adjusted the set of spectacles on his nose and peered into one pigeonhole after another, plucking out something here and something else there until he had three envelopes in hand.

John always did that. Jug would've thought the easy way to do things would be to bunch all the mail going to any one outfit into one place so it could be taken out and handed over all at one time, but John had his own system of placing things in the tall mail case he'd had built.

"Is William Knott still working out there?" John asked, chin tucked low so he could see over the top of his eyeglasses.

"Who's that?"

John looked down to the letters. "I have a letter here for William Knott. It's addressed to him at the M Bar C. The letter comes from Stuttgart, Arkansas."

"Wil— oh, you mean Billy."

"Says William on this letter here."

"Billy the kid is what we call him." Jug grinned. "Never thought of him as having a whole name, but I expect he'd have to. Yeah, he's still there. Doing pretty good now, too."

"In that case, I think this is everything for you." John handed the thin sheaf of letters through the window. "Is there anything else I can do for you?"

"No, I expect not, but I thank you."

John took up the little wooden CLOSED sign and placed it in the post office window with meticulous care, then stepped out from behind the wall that separated the post office's business from the store. "Can I interest you in some shirts, Jug? I have a new supply since you were here. Very nice."

John was always careful about that sort of thing. Wouldn't so much as mention store business while he was standing inside the post office area although he didn't mind answering post office questions while he was in the merchandise part of the place.

"No thank you, Mr. Cade."

"Let me know if you change your mind."

"Yes, sir, I will. Thank you." Jug folded the envelopes in half and tried to stick them into his vest pocket where Eli's lists had been but they were too big to fit. He stuffed them into his left side hip pocket instead. The right side was reserved for his gloves. Like any working cowboy who depended on ropes and roping for a living, he protected his hands and wouldn't have been comfortable stepping outside in the morning without his gloves. He'd as soon have forgotten his gloves as his hat, and he couldn't have moved a step outdoors without his hat any more than he could've left his boots behind. Of course, some of the boys these days liked to stick their gloves in the waistbands of their britches but Jug thought that was ostentatious, showing them like that. He liked to keep things simple. Always had.

Jug stepped outside and glanced down to the ground. The shadows were growing long. There wasn't much daylight left. Not that he needed daylight to find his way back. Not hardly.

Now that his errands were all done, Jug figured he could take a little time for himself. Get something to fill his belly and, why not, maybe a little something to wet his whistle, too.

He adjusted the tilt of his battered and sweat-stained old hat to a more jaunty angle and sauntered off down the street toward Anna Chong's Chop House.

11

A visitor passing through Bonner might get himself something of a surprise if he stepped into Anna Chong's looking for a pork chop or a lamb chop or some such cut of tender meat. Over in Cheyenne or back east and places like that a restaurant called a chophouse was a classy sort of place and generally a pricey one, too.

Anna's wasn't like that.

At Anna's the "chop" stood for chop suey, and it was the cheapest place in town for a store-bought meal. Ten cents for a big bowl of Anna's vegetable-laden and aromatic chop suey. Nickel for a refill, and all the rice a fellow could hold came along free.

Jug had no idea how or where Anna found all the fresh, crunchy vegetables to make her chop suey, but even in wintertime she'd get them brought in from someplace. He'd gotten to like the stuff so much that he ate at Anna's even when he wasn't close to being broke. Of course right now, it being so long since payday, he was close enough to broke that eating at Anna's was doubly sensible.

He finished off the one bowl and a heap of rice and had a drink of water instead of paying for coffee. If he was going to buy a beverage it wasn't going to be coffee. Then he went outside with the warmth of a hot meal spreading through his middle and feeling pretty good, his game leg notwithstanding.

The Bullhorn saloon was only a couple blocks away. It was a quiet place. Friendly. Jug had been stopping in there, time to time, as long as he'd been in this country.

A few years back when Carl Emant sold the Bullhorn and went back east to live with a daughter there was something of a furor about the place. Gerald Fulbright bought it and one of the first things he did was hang a big sign out front. It was a Bull Durham sign that Gerald repainted so it said BULL-HORN instead of Bull Durham. That part nobody minded, but there was an uproar because it was pretty plain that it was indeed a bull that was depicted, right out there where everyone including ladies and young girls could see.

There was preaching from the pulpit to

denounce the lewdness — or so Jug was told; he hadn't actually been on hand to hear that for himself — and it was even brought up in a town council meeting.

Gerald settled the problem with a dab of paint that made the bull on his sign into a steer. Then he showed a streak of independence by getting another sign and putting it inside where only the gents could see.

The way Jug saw it, the outside sign was kinda appropriate anyway despite the name of the place because inside the huge old walnut backbar had a six-foot-wide set of horns mounted on it and impressive as those horns were, anybody who knew cattle also knew that they'd come off a steer and not a bull as it was only the steers of the longhorn breed that grew really big sets of horn.

Some of the younger hands and certainly the townsfolk, though, wouldn't likely know that. There hadn't been a genuine longhorn in this country since God knew when. They'd all been sold off as cheap beef to make way for the heavier bodied and therefore more profitable newfangled bloodlines. Once the buyers started paying by the pound instead of the head — which they'd done so they could buy western beeves cheaper and try to gouge the stockmen —

the day of the old-time longhorn was done.

Jug kind of missed them. They'd been mean and spooky and quick as cats, hard to work and harder to drive. But he'd admired them for all their faults, and he was sorry they were gone now.

"Whiskey for you today, Jug?" Tabe Evans asked when Jug stepped up to the bar and staked out a claim there with an elbow propped in place.

"Not this time of month. Gimme a beer, if you please."

"One beer for the gentleman with the smile," Tabe said and turned away to fetch a clean mug off the pyramid of glassware and draw a fresh one.

12

Oh, hell. Willis Johnston was drunk. Nice fella, Willis. Mostly. Rode for the K5T brand. Big, strong ol' boy. Friendly. Except when he was drunk. Willis was hell on wheels when he'd tipped a few too many. This evening he'd definitely had himself too many.

"Sing, boys, sing," Willis roared, although not any louder than your average tornado. "Sing 'Pop Goes the Weasel,' boys. Loud now. I can't hear you."

Which seemed pretty reasonable considering that no one, including Willis, was singing.

Willis eyeballed some of the other fellows at the bar, then spied Jug standing innocent — and silent — a couple feet away from him.

"Dammit, Jug, you ain't singing." Willis shouted the comment as if Jug was in the next county south instead of standing right there.

"That's right, Willis, I ain't."

Willis blinked owlishly. "You too good t' sing with me, Jug?"

"Don't know the words, Willis." Which was true enough. Not that singing with a drunk seemed such a good idea to start with, but in fact he did *not* know the words to "Pop Goes the Weasel."

"What the hell do you know then?" Willis demanded.

Jug shrugged and turned his back, hoping to break off this conversation before things got out of hand. Could be it was a mistake to turn away, though. Considering.

Jug felt Willis's big ol' hand whack down — hard — on top of his right shoulder and spin him back around to face the big K5T cowboy. "Dammit, Willis, that hurt."

"You gonna sing with me, Jug, or ain't you?"

"Ain't," Jug said.

"I'll thump you, Jug. You know I mean it. I'll thump you good if you don't sing with me."

"You're drunk, Willis. Go home. Sleep it off."

"I'm gonna count to three, Jug. If you don't sing with me I'll thump you good."

Jug tipped his head back — had to tilt it quite a ways back, actually — and squinted with one eye half shut while he gave Willis a critical examination. Willis was somebody Jug'd never fought before, and of the grown men in and around Bonner that was something of a rarity. Cowboys tend to protect their hands from damage, but there are some exceptions to that rule and Jug never had been one to back off from a fight. And besides, by now he'd had three or four beers himself, so while he wasn't drunk like Willis he wasn't entirely cold sober either.

"You can't fight Jug, Willis," Tabe Evans put in from his side of the bar. "You're a head and a half taller than him."

Which was not much of an exaggeration. Willis probably stood six feet two and would weigh in at two hundred thirty, maybe two hundred forty pounds. Jug was five four and had to keep his boots on to make a hundred twenty.

"You hush up, Tabe. Jug, I'm countin' now. One . . . two . . ."

Jug didn't see any point to waiting for Willis to take the first shot. He brought his right fist in low and just as hard as he could throw it, aiming just below Willis's belt buckle. It wasn't low enough to be a dirty blow and thus cause a sure enough blood feud between them, but he wanted it low enough to drive out every scrap of air Willis'd been able to breathe in for the past week or so.

Willis went pale, doubled over, and commenced to puking on the Bullhorn floor.

Jug, for his part, had gone and forgotten in the excitement of the moment that he didn't have much of a left leg under him. And he'd put every ounce of his weight onto that leg so he could get the leverage to stop this fight before it got out of hand.

The leg just wasn't quite up to that sort of use just yet and it buckled, sending Jug reeling off balance. He twisted into contortions a medicine show artiste would've envied in his attempts to avoid Willis's vomit, bounced off the front of the Bullhorn bar, and went down. Hard.

He fell on his left side — naturally, it being his left leg that gave out under him — and to add insult to injury landed half on and half off one of the cuspidors that were placed along the front of the bar.

It might've been better if he'd landed all the way on the brass spittoon because the glancing blow he gave it not only hurt like hell, it also caused it to overturn. And spill.

Jug felt cold spit and used tobacco juice flood his britches and wondered if he'd have been better off letting Willis thump him.

Not that he had much of a choice about it now.

He rolled aside quick as a cat — just in case Willis wasn't so far out of the fray as Jug hoped and intended — but had to crawl on his knees to one of the nearby tables and grab hold of a chair so he could drag himself upright again.

He needn't have worried. Willis was still on his knees examining what he'd eaten for lunch earlier that day.

"You all right, Jug?"

"I'm all right, Tabe." It was wishful thinking but at least his outlook was positive. Truth was he hurt like hell.

Tabe kinda grinned, and, Gary McCarthy, one of the too-dang-many spectators, laughed outright and said, "I swear, Jug, that's the first time I've seen a one-punch fight end with both fellas knocked down."

Jug was about to wipe some of the mess off his britches, then remembered what it was he'd sat in and decided to leave things be until he could get his pants off and get them cleaned.

"Willis." Willis didn't answer. "Willis, are you listening to me?" Willis didn't so much as look in his direction.

"It's all right, Jug," McCarthy said. "Willis don't carry a grudge."

"Lordy, I hope not," Jug admitted. "I couldn't sucker him a second time."

"Hell, maybe you could. I said the man won't grudge you. I never claimed he's bright."

Jug laughed and shuffled out of the Bullhorn, trying not to show a limp as he did so.

He was hoping it was still early enough that he could catch the Chinese laundry open so he could get a quick wash for his britches. He purely hated the idea of riding all the way back to the M Bar C with his butt full of other people's spit.

13

It was embarrassing is what it was. There Jug stood, wrapped in an old blanket, while folks — decent female folks even — came and went. Had to be done though. It takes some time to wash a pair of nastied-on britches and get them halfway dry again. He knew that. He just didn't like having to stand here like a cigar store Indian while it was being done, that was all.

He must have been there the better part of two hours before Lily gave him one of her huge, gap-toothed grins and waved his pants high to show him they were ready. Lily wasn't her actual name. That was understood. But no one in Bonner except for Anna Chong and Lily's husband and cousins could pronounce her right name, and they'd all gotten so accustomed to the name Lily that it would have been impossible now to think of her as anything else. Lily was always smiling, always friendly.

Jug grabbed his pants and went slinking off to one side of the little storefront, hoping nobody would come in and observe this procedure, so he could hold the blanket in place with one hand and struggle into his pants with the other.

The cloth was hot from being ironed. That was the way they'd hurried up the drying process of course, ironing and ironing and ironing them to drive the moisture out. It worked pretty well, too, although they still felt damp. Clean damp, though, so that was all right. And hot. The heat felt kinda good to him, then less so as the heat quickly dissipated and the dampness began to feel clammy. Even that was okay compared to the feeling he'd had before, of course.

"Ten cen'," Lily told him and he gladly paid. Would've paid ten times that to get rid of the mess from the Bullhorn.

He thanked her and started for the door.

"You wai'."

"Huh?"

"Wai' he." Her hand gestures told him this meant "wait here." Lily's English was not perfect. On the other hand, it was a helluva lot better than Jug's Chinese and he didn't figure he was in any position to criticize anybody else's linguistic abilities when he himself had none at all.

He had his britches and he'd already paid, but if Lily wanted him to wait here, well . . .

She ran into the back of the laundry with that odd little short-step run she had and re-emerged a moment later carrying some papers.

Jug couldn't figure what that was about until he saw that she had some envelopes, too. Then he remembered. He'd had the outfit's letters in his back pocket. They must've gotten drenched right along with everything else back there. He hoped they could still be read.

And there sure seemed a lot of them. There'd only been, what? Four letters. The one to Billy and the rest addressed to the foreman. Lily handed him four envelopes and at least a dozen sheets of paper. Maybe more. They were smudged and the ink faded just about clean away in some spots.

Lily or one of them in the back had tried to salvage things as best they could. They'd gone to the trouble of ironing the paper, too, to try to dry it. The creases where the paper was folded to go into the envelopes were ironed out and the paper sheets had a brittle feel to them from the ironing, but they were in better shape than they should have been.

"Lily, that's mighty nice o' you. Thanks."

He dug into his pocket for more coins, but Lily waved the offer away. "No mo'. Pan' only." She sure wasn't big on the letter "t." It occurred to Jug that one of these days he'd have to see if he could inveigle Lily into saying "tip-top Hottentot" just to see how she'd handle it.

He thanked her again and made a mental note to himself that he owed her and her kin a kindness, and he'd have to remember to do something nice for them sometime. Finding unexpected goodness in folks always tickled him, and this example went a long way toward brightening what could have seemed a rather sour ending to a long day.

He thanked Lily one more time with a tip of his hat and a grin that was near about as gap-toothed as hers and went off to find that slow — but steady, oh yes, steady — old Lady Horse for the trip home.

It would be late when he got there, but what the heck. He'd just take a wrap on the horn with his reins and sleep most of the way.

14

Jug was feeling pretty good. Thanks to that plodding old hunk of walking horsemeat he'd gotten a pretty good sleep last night — a heckuva lot more than if he'd been on night watch with a trail herd out in the Big Empty somewhere — and this morning he felt so darn chipper that he was attempting actual biscuits.

Generally his breakfasts consisted of coffee, bacon, and whatever was left over from the night before. If anything was left over, that is.

Complicated cooking was not exactly his best thing. Beans you just soak and then boil and maybe cut in some pieces of bacon and onion if you have any, to add a bit of flavor. Bacon you only have to slice and fry. And coffee, well, you simply get your pot of water to boiling and then dump in a couple handsful of ground coffee. Handful of coffee for every quart of water. That was the rule of thumb. Worked out all right, too.

This morning, though, this morning he was taking a crack at biscuits. He did dearly love his biscuits and woke up wanting some. Never been successful at making any, but he'd seen it done. And how hard could it be to make a little ol' biscuit anyway?

Jug got his ingredients out and mixed everything together and spoon-dropped the dough onto a metal sheet. He put that in the oven with the fire stoked up nice and hot, then sat back with a cup of weak, half-boiled coffee to wait for the biscuits to be ready and the foreman to get there.

A crinkly sound coming out of his back pocket reminded him of the letters he'd folded over and stuffed in there last night. He'd forgotten about them. He pulled them out and decided while he was waiting for breakfast to happen he'd see could he sort out what papers went into which envelopes so Eli wouldn't wind up with Billy the kid's letter from home nor Billy try to figure out why his mama was sending him instructions on how she wanted the ranch run.

He turned the wick on the lamp higher and held the papers out in front of him, then smoothed them and pushed them out a little further so he could make out the words. Funny thing, but he was having to

15

"You know, Jug, these ones that are raw on the inside aren't so bad. At least you can break into them without needing the ax." Eli paused and when Jug didn't say anything added, "Should I be expecting a visit from the sheriff?"

Jug jumped a little, startled, and gave the foreman a wide-eyed stare. "What d'you mean by that?"

"I mean, did you get yourself into some trouble when you were in town yesterday, that's what I mean."

Jug shook his head and went back to morosely peering into his plate as if the cold bacon lying there could be read like a fortune teller's tea leaves.

"Then what's wrong with you this morning, Jug? You haven't hardly touched your food . . . not that a well man would want to . . . and you haven't smiled nor said scarcely a word. Something's bothering you. Got a bellyache or something?"

"Something. Let it go at that."

"If you say so. It's your horse to ride. I just thought I'd ask." He sounded a little peeved to have made the overture only to be rejected. Eli gave up on the biscuits — which were on the verge of being inedible. For that matter, some of them were almost to the point of being unbreakable — hard and scorched almost black. He went back to his bacon and coffee.

Jug continued jabbing his fork at the same piece of bacon he'd been chasing around his plate practically since he sat down. After a while he quit pretending to eat and tried the coffee. It was cold and bitter so he went to the door and threw that cup out, then went back and poured a hot cup from the pot. He didn't rejoin Poole at the table though, instead busying himself with getting hot water from the oven reservoir and slicing small, curly slivers of yellow all-purpose naphtha soap into a basin so he could start washing up after the meal.

The foreman's eyes drilled a few holes into Jug's back and soon he picked up his mail and left, leaving his plate and cup on the table for Jug to clean up.

16

It kept rolling over and over through his mind like one of those penny arcade things. You crank the handle and the wheel of cards spins around and around so that you see them so fast they look like it's one card with the figures moving and no end to it at all, so if you kept on cranking the figures would do those same things over and over and over again. Except this time it wasn't some cowboy roping the same steer over and over or a hansom cab driving down a lane in Central Park in New York City but words that Jug kept seeing roll through his mind.

Winter kill. Those were the words he saw the most. *Winter kill.* And a figure. One hundred forty-eight. Written out just like that, too. The man who wrote the letter wrote the number out clear as could be.

Jug kept wondering to himself if maybe he hadn't got it right. If maybe somehow he'd misread what he saw on that sheet. If maybe the ink was so blurred that he was wrong. Except if it had been figures he'd seen there, like 148 instead of the written-out words, he could've convinced himself that the letter writer meant dollars lost and not head lost. Maybe.

But it wasn't so. It wasn't like that at all. The writer wrote the numbers out in script, and he sure hadn't been talking about money lost but about cows. Winter killed cows. Jug saw it for himself right there on that page. One hundred forty-eight head of winter kill cows.

Jug hadn't gone through and read the whole letter. Wasn't sent to him and he hadn't meant to read any of it.

Now he wished that he had. A hundred forty-eight head of winter kill.

There hadn't been that much winter kill on the M Bar C since, well since he didn't know when. Even back during what they were now calling the Big Die-Up — back in the winter of '87 to '88 when the eastern part of Wyoming and western Nebraska and Dakota and down into parts of Colorado, back when the blizzards came and wouldn't quit and everybody in the cow business like to got wiped out by winter kill — even back then the M Bar C hadn't lost that many cows, seeing as the outfit was protected from the worst of the snow and the wind by the Sheephorns lying to the west of them.

The storms that terrible winter came whooshing over the top of the Sheephorns and the wind didn't curl back down to ground level until it got over to the Camus Range or thereabouts so that the whole of the Hayden Creek valley was pretty much spared from the die-up that ruined so many other outfits off to the east and the south.

That was the year, those were the storms, that warned the surviving outfits about winter feeding for their beeves. That was the year that haying and winter feeding came to be in a big way in this whole stretch of northern plains country from the Arkansas River on up into Canada or God knew where.

If they'd had hay to feed that year the hard-hit outfits out east would've weathered over fairly well. Would've saved an awful lot of beeves that ended up dead and frozen with no value except their hides and those only if the carcasses could be got to before bad rot set in.

That had been a good year for wolves or coyotes and a bad one for cattlemen.

But the cattlemen learned, and now they put up hay for winter feeding so such an awful thing as that wouldn't be repeated.

Winter kill. Jug doubted the M Bar C had lost a hundred forty-eight head to winter kill over the past five years combined, never mind in just this one winter past.

For a moment there he brightened. Could've been the letter writer was commenting on some aggregate number. A five-year figure. Or ten. Would they've lost a hundred forty-eight over the past ten years?

Jug tried to tote it up in his mind, but the truth was that he'd lost track of the winter kill numbers from some of those years. Hadn't been his job to keep track of them anyway, but a man kind of pays attention to the herd and tends to know what cows are missing or what ones had full bags but no calves beside them so as to indicate the calf losses.

He just couldn't remember them all. Not right off.

He was damn sure though that this past year's loss had been light. Three grown cows that he knew of . . . and those had been old cattle that were weak and aged going into the winter . . . and four, maybe five calves born too early to survive the harsh winds and sometimes bitter temperatures.

Eight head, call it. Eight. Could've been a couple more than that. Maybe. But . . . *a hundred forty* more?

No, ma'am. A hundred forty-eight head winter killed would've been a catastrophe that had the whole country talking.

The M Bar C could survive a loss like that, he supposed. But . . . a hundred forty-eight head? Didn't happen. Hardly *could* happen.

So why was the letter writer from back east writing something to Eli about a hundred forty-eight head of winter kill?

The thought was deviling Jug and he just couldn't let it be. He wished now he'd gone ahead and read through the rest of that letter.

Wished he'd gone and done that or . . . or something. He didn't know what.

Dammit, he wished he didn't know anything about this. Wasn't any of his never-mind to start with.

All he was supposed to do was to get up in the morning and saddle a horse, go out and do whatever work was required of him, and come nightfall go to bed to get ready to do it all over again come the morrow.

That was all a cowboy did or was supposed to do. He damn sure wasn't expected to fret about things that were outside his job. He *knew* that.

Jug sighed. Damn words kept chewing inside his belly anyway.

One hundred forty-eight head. Winter killed.

Jug snorted once, loudly, then went about washing up the dishes and stuff he'd used to commit the crime of biscuits this morning.

17

" 'Lo, Jug."

" 'Lo yourself, Bernie."

"Is that coffee I smell?"

"Ayuh, help yourself. I made plenty."

Bernie Randall stripped off his gloves and reached for a cup. He smelled the brew before he drank, then smacked his lips and said, "It isn't Coosie's, but it beats hell out of a bellyful of crick water, which is what I had for lunch. Didn't think to carry any food along. Is that some leftovers from lunch?"

Without waiting for an answer, Bernie grabbed a plate and a spoon and began loading up with last night's beans that Jug recooked today with some molasses and onion chunks added to them to make them a little different this time around.

"Damn, Jug. This here's pretty good," he mumbled around the first mouthful.

"Dig right in. Have all you want."

It was clear that Bernie intended to do

exactly that. And after all, there was plenty of everything. For the past week and a half Jug had been cooking enough to serve at least two, but Eli hadn't eaten with him in the cookhouse since the morning Jug made those awful biscuits. And delivered that mail.

Not that either one of them had said a word about the letters from back east. But the foreman hadn't come to a meal again since then. He would wander over about half-past breakfast and grab a cup of coffee while he laid out Jug's work for the day. Then he would disappear, sometimes into the main house where he had taken to sleeping this past year or so or he would saddle a horse and ride off someplace.

It kind of tickled Jug to note that when Eli took off like that he would choose any direction at all. Except one. He never, *ever* rode off toward the Goodrun place.

"What'd you come in for, Bernie?" Jug asked his unexpected visitor.

"Jesse sent me on ahead to let the foreman know we're about finished with the gather. He wants to know should he cut the herd out there or bring the whole bunch down."

Jug nodded. Jesse's judgment on the subject would be at least as good as Eli's, but Eli was the foreman and not Jesse. Asking was the right thing to do although either one of them could read the grass and the calendar and the weather and come up with the right answers to that and a couple hundred other questions.

For that matter, Jug and a good many of the other fellows could do the same if they wanted to. In Jug's case, he didn't want to.

"About done with working 'em?" Jug asked.

"Yeah, just about. They were gonna make one more gather today. You know the draw above where that Injun burial platform used to be?"

Jug knew it. When he first came to this country you could still see the warped and weathered poles where the platform collapsed after nobody knew how many years. There weren't any bones left or anything else that a body might want for a souvenir, but a little bit of the platform had been intact then. The amazement to him was that any hand on the outfit and probably most of the fellows working anyplace this side of Hayden Creek would also know that spot. Most of them, Bernie included, came into the country years after the last visible traces of that old burial platform disappeared. But they all knew where it had been and could relate directions based on that knowledge. So yeah, he knew exactly the draw Bernie meant.

"They were gonna work that today, then if they had some daylight left start the herd. Get 'em away from the hills and the brush so they wouldn't be so likely to try an' break out."

Jug glanced toward the sky, purely a reflexive habit since they were indoors and he sure couldn't see the sun's position from in here, and decided they would already be moving toward the home place if they were going to at all today. He was already pretty sure about the general time of day anyhow. "Got any notion what you'd like for supper, Bernie?"

"Biscuits. I'd like me some biscuits," Randall declared.

Jug grinned. "That's good. Make enough for me, too." He handed Bernie the water bucket he'd been about to fill when the cowboy arrived, then walked out quick before Bernie could squawk.

18

Jug's leg still hurt like hell but at least he could step onto a horse like a white man again, left leg first, and not have to use a stump to climb on with.

It still hurt some to ride, but then it hurt some, too, to lie in his own dang bunk if he rolled over wrong.

And he'd sure rather be mounted and feeling like he was accomplishing something than lying on some stupid bunk in broad daylight.

When the herd came down, Jug was there waiting for them and was able to help keep them buched while other more fit and agile hands did the much harder physical work of cutting and mugging and branding.

Jug couldn't have handled the jarring spins and cutbacks of a horse intent on cutting spooky and unwilling calves from the herd, and he damn sure couldn't manage the dismounted chores involved with throwing and branding and castrating. The leg was far from being ready for that yet.

Like always, they started out on a nice patch of green grass and next thing you knew all that grass had either been eaten or trampled so by the end of the day what you had left was dirt and dust, dirt and dust being two of the constants in any cowhand's life. Well, those plus horses and cows. Couldn't run beeves without those four things plus one other irreplaceable ingredient — that being the cowboy himself.

Jug had heard it said that cowboys were mostly made up of dirt and dust, likely from having eaten so much of both, which perhaps explained why they weren't as smart as either their horses or the cows. Not that Jug believed this. But he'd heard it said.

"Jug!"

"Yeah, boss." He'd've been damned if he'd ever call Eli Poole that, but somehow he didn't mind it when it was Jesse he was talking to.

"You can ride back and tell Coosie we'll be in a little short of sundown this evening, and we'll be hungry as a bunch of grizzlies in February when we get there."

"Who's on night herd?"

"We'll bring the culls in an' pen them in the big horse trap. Start keeping them separate ready to trail them down to the railroad when this workin' is done. Only have to night herd the main bunch that way. I figure the kid and Randall can take first watch, then Roger Mullen and the Polack for the second half."

"What about me, dammit?"

"You're still stove up, Jug. I can see it in your face. You're hurting. Be plenty of time for you to lose sleep when your leg is feeling better."

"I haven't been pulling my weight, Jesse, and there's no reason I can't ease around on a nice, slow night watch."

"Nobody begrudges you, Jug."

"Didn't say anybody does, but I don't feel right drawing wages and stuffing my belly and not doing any work."

"All right, you can take the kid's place on first watch. Go tell him I said he's to ride in an' let Coosie knew when we'll be along."

"That's fine."

"You're a stubborn old fart, Jeremiah Ulysses Gordon."

Jug looked around to see no one else was nearby.

"Oh hell, Jug, I didn't say it where anybody could hear." Jesse grinned and spat, barely missing the scuffed and manure-stained toe of his left boot. He knew perfectly good and well that Jug didn't want anyone to know his proper name.

Jug tried to give Jesse a look of withering menace but managed only a poor imitation that brought a rip of laughter out of the segundo's belly. "Go on now, dammit. We still got work t' do here."

Jug kneed his horse forward.

"And don't forget to tell the kid," Jesse called after him. "If this bunch finds nothing but cold leftovers for supper when they get in this evening it'll be your fault, and don't think I won't tell them so."

Jug made a rather vulgar gesture in the segundo's direction, then with a grimace put his mount into a trot as he went to find Billy the kid and deliver the instructions. The gait hurt but damned if he'd let Jesse see that.

After a couple rods at that rough, ground-pounding trot, he used the ends of his reins to quirt the horse into a lope, which was infinitely more comfortable to sit.

19

Yee-haw! Jug didn't holler it out loud. But he felt it inside his belly.

This here, this was all right. Made a man sit tall and feel good, by gum.

Oh, it wasn't a pimple on a gnat's butt to the old days when a man could push three, four thousand head of beeves at a time and drive them for months on end. Those were the days, all right.

But this, this was good enough and better than most had it in these times of railroad tracks and boxcars reaching here, there, and everywhere through the whole of the west.

The time was come — Jug had no idea in the world how the owners and owner reps decided on an exact date so far in advance when they couldn't know how the weather and the grass and all would turn out to be — this was the time when every outfit in the basin would gather together with their spring crop. They'd put all the culled steers from a dozen brands — more if you counted those pipsqueak little spit-and-rawhide outfits in the north — into one big road herd and drive them down to the railroad at Tie Siding.

Jug was told — he hadn't been in this country at the time, mind — that Tie Siding started out because somebody had a contract to cut, cure, and deliver crossties for the railroad that was being built at the time. Whoever it was must have done a good job of it for there wasn't a decent stand of trees within ten miles now, but who knew what it might've been like that far back.

In any event, or so the story went, the railroad put a siding in so the supply trains could get out of the way of the main line and let the work trains through. Then somebody else came along and put up some pens and loading chutes, and now the pens served beef outfits for a hundred miles north of the siding and probably about as far to the south, too.

Spring and fall, the stockmen would load their beeves onto railcars and ship them east to sell. Springtime they sold fewer cattle, but the prices were higher seeing as how there hadn't been all that much beef available to the packing houses through the winter. Fall the prices weren't quite so good per pound but the steers were fatter from their summer grazing and there were more of them on the market. That was because every beeve you carried over until spring had to be fed through the winter. It made for an interesting juggling act, trying to decide how many to market when. And it was why ranchers and their foremen got gray hair earlier than their cowhands did.

Not that Jug had to worry about going gray. He was near enough to bald that the color didn't hardly seem to matter.

Now though, now they were fixing to get out and go. Gather and push maybe five or six hundred head.

Over the years, this spring drive had become about as much a social event as a business necessity. It was an easy drive, seeing as the grass wasn't tall yet and the cattle not terribly strong, so they had to take things slow anyway. Tradition had it that the owners, those who lived in the basin, would all come along, and generally they brought their sons and their sons' pals so the yonkers could get a taste of the trail driving they would've heard so much about.

They let the boys out of school and any of them big enough to swing a rope would try to wheedle permission to join in on the fun.

Jug had no idea what the wives and the

little girls back home did during this time, but he suspected they'd have a good time of it, too, doing whatever it is that little girls and respectable womenfolk do.

They'd take a couple days to get from the M Bar C down to the holding grounds below Bonner where the trail herd would come together. Then it'd be another couple weeks of slow driving to move them all down to the pens at Tie Siding.

Oh, it was grand, it was, and Jug was feeling much better now that his leg was on the mend. He felt practically back to his old self again and was eager to start.

Yessir. This was a red-letter, yee-haw day for dang sure.

20

This was droving at its best. The grass was young and tender so that the beeves couldn't hardly get their fill of it. The group was drifting along slow and easy so the animals would put on weight. Cows, horses . . . people, too.

Every outfit had its own trail cook along and part of the occasion was that each brand tried to outdo every other as to the meal fixings. Jug doubted they would've eaten better if they'd tied on the feedbag at the finest restaurants in Cheyenne. No bacon and beans for this trip. No, sir. On the spring drive it was more apt to be ham, turkey, or fried chicken, the birds being brought in special just for this.

The F R Bar, being British owned and therefore considering itself more than a little hoity-toity, went so far as to order a barrel of passenger pigeons, which the cook claimed should be called *squab* but which everybody knew right off was really passenger pigeon. Whatever anybody wanted to call it, it was tasty and then some.

Evenings the fellows would wander from chuckwagon to cook tent, everyone free to sample whatever was on hand. The cooks always prepared enough for their own outfits and about half the rest of the oversized crowd. And there never seemed to be any food go to waste.

Days the outfits would rotate positions with the herd so that one day a brand and its riders would be on point. The next day they'd be riding drag, and the day after that they'd move up alongside the bunch.

At this time of year and with no larger a herd than they had to tear up the grass there wasn't hardly any dust to swallow, even back in drag. Now on one of those big, miles-long, old-timey heards . . . a man came to know dust when he rode drag back then. Jug knew. He'd sure gobbled down his share of the stuff. Not now though. No, sir.

Easy days. Peaceful nights. This was a fine way to drive cattle.

"Jug."

"Yeah, Jesse? You want me on night herd?" He knew better, of course. That was another nice thing about this social turnout of a spring drive. They carried along so many hands, including a dozen or more young-sters eager to prove themselves on horse-back, that the older fellows didn't have to stand night herd. That, too, was part of the tradition that was growing in the basin.

The segundo snickered and tilted his head in the direction of a roaring bonfire with a gang of bodies gathered close around it. "They're telling ghost stories over there. Whyn't you tell them your Texas pirate yarn?"

"Aw, they've all of 'em heard that one too many times, Jesse."

"Got to be five, six young'uns over there making their first trip, Jug. Be a damn shame for 'em to miss out on the pirate."

Jug grinned. "If you say so."

Jesse didn't say anything more. But he did walk with Jug over to the fire where Pete Holcomb from the Circle B was finishing up a tale.

Jug sucked the last shreds of meat off a chicken leg and tossed the bone to one of the dogs that'd come along for the fun, then stepped into the middle of the circle of firelight when Pete was done.

"The pirate, Mr. Jug, tell us the one about the pirate." A chorus of pleas rose from some of the older boys, yonkers who were on their second or third trip down to the

Siding. "Tell us the pirate. Please."

"All right then. But mind you, this is no made-up ghost story. This is something that actually happened down in Texas where I was raised. Now this was along Matagorda Bay, you see, and back in the olden days there was lots of pirates put into the bay to hide from the law. They buried treasure there, it's said, and some of them yet haunt the places where their treasure is lost. But this ain't about treasure, boys. This is about a pirate . . . nobody alive knows what his name was . . . who had only one hand. Had him an iron hook where his left hand shoulda been. And it's said that what he liked best was to find young'uns . . . a boy an' a girl out sparking in the moonlight is what he liked best . . . and . . ."

Jug's voice rose and fell. He stalked an imaginary foe before his wide-eyed audience — the younger the boy the wider the eyes, it seemed — and whirled, stamped, cooed softly to a nonexistent buggy horse, threw himself into the role he was acting out for his story.

"Tommy felt a chill in the air and smelled something like the stink of a moldy grave . . . he told me this his own self, mind . . . and whatever was there in the night spooked the horse so that they took off with a jerk that threw Amy off the seat and onto the floor of the buggy.

"That horse must've run three quarters of a mile, Tommy told me, before he could get the poor, shiverin' critter to calm down and drop back to a walk. By then Amy's dress was all mussed and she was fretting about what her mama was gonna say when they got home, so Tommy drove her straight back to town.

"And d'you know what they found when they parked out front of her daddy's store and Tommy went around to hand her down off the buggy? D'you know?"

"Tell us, Mr. Jug."

"What did they find, Mr. Jug?"

"It was an iron hook, boys. An iron hook with a padded cuff like what would fit over a pirate's stump. That's what they found. It was hanging there, caught in the bows of the buggy top and ripped off the pirate's arm when the horse spooked and run off like it did. That's what they found, boys, strike me down dead from the sky if that isn't the natural truth."

Whenever he told this story, Jug was very careful to avoid inviting God his own self to do the striking, though.

Just in case.

The boys whispered among themselves,

the young ones more than likely turning to their elders to see if the yarn really could be so.

Jug never took part in any of that. He tipped his hat to the kids and stepped quietly out of the firelight to rejoin Jesse and some of the fellows. Rumor had it that the Polack had a bottle to share around, and while nobody would've considered getting actual drunk on these spring drives a wee nip now and then was considered well within the bounds of fun and good fellowship.

21

"Why is a steer's horn bigger than a bull's, Mr. Jug?"

Jug had no idea why. It was so, that was all. So he made one up. Had to have an answer for a kid's question, after all. "It's because a steer's strength can't go where it natural would, like in a bull, so it comes out in his horn. Got t' go somewhere, don't you see."

"But a cow's horn is short like a bull's."

"Yes and that proves what I'm telling you. We don't alter heifers, do we?"

"No, sir."

"My point exactly. Now keep your eyes on that droopy horn critter over there. See how his eyes are rolling? He's fixing to make a run out of the bunch. Be ready to turn him back when he does."

"Me, Mr. Jug? You want me to do it?"

He snorted. "Course I do. You can do it good as I can so why should I rattle my poor old bones?"

Jug grinned a couple minutes later when the droopy horn steer snorted and made his dash. The kid — Jug couldn't recall what this one's name was — did just fine at turning him straight back into the herd. When he rode back beside Jug the kid — Tim, that was his name Jug minded now — was proud as if he'd accomplished something grand.

And in a way maybe he had at that.

"No, not so steep an angle as that. Like this." Jug reached over and turned the boy's wrist just a bit so as to adjust the way the knife blade lay against the scrap of fine grit Carborundum cloth the boy was using to sharpen his knife. Or trying to. He wasn't very adept at it.

"I'll never learn."

"Course you will, Albert. Nobody starts off knowing everything. You got to learn. Now look. See the angle here? It's got t' be just so. Shallower than that, like this, say, and you get a real sharp edge, but it's thin. Won't last a minute if you go to cutting or whittling at something. Fine edge like that will curl and dull the steel quick as if 'twas paper.

"You don't want t' hold it upright like this neither. Like this. See how I mean? You hold it too tall like that and it takes too broad an edge. That kinda edge lasts longer but it won't cut clean and easy. Might as well use a flat stick as an edge like that.

"But you hold your blade like this. You see what I mean? That's right, just like that. An' you'll put a nice edge on. But go slow an' be patient. Slow and patient are what you want here. Don't wanta get the metal too hot from rubbing an' you want the angle just . . . that's it, Albert. Just like that. Then keep dragging it acrost the cloth. One way, then t'other. You're doing fine, son."

"No, son, you're putting too big a handle on that loop. Shorten up a little. That's right. Now whirl 'er around just once to open 'er up and throw like I taught you." Jug clapped his hands and bawled, "Good throw, son. Perfect," when the boy's loop by some miracle dropped over the weathered old buffalo skull Jug set atop a stake for the kids to use as a roping dummy.

Lordy, they did come flocking to him of an evening when the herd was bedded and the smell of supper and woodsmoke enticing on the breeze.

Jug liked it. For the first couple years he'd wondered why it was he was the one they always picked to come pester with their questions and their lessons. Then he'd figured it out. Or thought he did.

He had time for them. More to the point, he took that time with them. Their daddies were mostly busy with one thing or another. Most of the hands didn't want to be bothered. The cooks damn sure didn't. Jug, he kinda enjoyed the young'uns. Questions and all.

One year after another it was like this, and he supposed by now he'd gotten close acquainted with just about every male human person in the basin from the age twenty-something on down to . . . the youngest this year was seven, he thought, or something like that.

"That's right. That's exactly right," he encouraged when the boy rebuilt his loop for another attempt at the buffalo skull.

22

The first sign Jug had that anything was amiss was when Tom Freeman approached him beside the loading pens. They'd reached Tie Siding shortly after midday and put the beeves into the pens easy. The cars were already there waiting to be loaded, which they'd do the next day, and there was a flatcar of hay delivered when the cattle cars were dropped off.

Some of the younger, more energetic hands were over on the flats beyond the tracks arranging some match races with their best ponies, and the pickup order for the cars to be hooked onto an eastbound train was already posted on the signal pole ready to be snatched up by the next locomotive to come roaring and clanking through.

Far as Jug knew everything was going mighty fine. He nodded a welcome to Freeman when the man approached him. Jug was standing with one boot hooked over a low rail, watching some of the middlin' sized kids try their hand at riding steers. A dozen or so of the smaller, lighter weight steers had been separated into a small enclosure for the boys to play with there.

" 'Lo, Tom," Jug said pleasantly. He didn't know Freeman all that well really. The man ran a little two-cow outfit — well, more or less — over on the east edge of the basin and did day work for anybody who needed an extra hand.

"I want a word with you, Jug."

"Sure thing, Tom." Jug dropped his boot to the ground and squared off to face the man. "You sound serious about something."

"I damn sure am that, mister." Freeman's face was red and his shoulders hunched and Jug had the idea he was about half a notion short of throwing a punch. That wasn't much like the little Jug knew about him. Freeman had the reputation for being an easygoing sort of fellow, sometimes too easygoing so that the ranchers who hired him on day wages took undue advantage. "I want you to stay away from my boy. Far away. D' you hear me? You keep your filthy self shut of him."

Jug blinked. Hard. Tom Freeman had a kid — the boy's name was Burt but everybody called him Birdie — who was ten, maybe eleven years old. He was one of the boys in the pen riding steers just now. Earlier this trip Jug had showed him how to whittle toy soldiers from willow shoots. Birdie said he wanted to make some for his sisters except he wouldn't call them soldiers then.

"I don't know what you mean, Tom, but . . ."

"Stay away from him, dammit. That's what I mean. Don't you so much as walk past a fire where my boy is sitting or I'll . . . I don't know what I'll do. Take a gun and settle for you if I have to. That's what I mean."

Freeman looked so mad Jug suspected he honestly didn't know what he intended.

"But what . . . ?"

Freeman didn't wait to hear out the question. He spun on his heels and marched away with a stiff-legged gait as if in a hurry to get clear before he lost control of himself.

Jug looked after him for a time. Then, shaking his head, he turned back to the pen where the kids were whooping and shouting and flying off the backs of frantically bucking steers.

The look on Tom Freeman's face stayed with him, though. Jug just wished he knew what in hell prompted that outburst.

23

"Jug."

"Yo."

"I need to see you."

Jug was busy at the moment. He was perched atop the rails at the foot of one of the loading chutes with a sharp stick where he could help control the movement of the steers being run up into a car. Beside the pen feeding beeves into the chute were the owners and their reps, busy making the final brand tally that would determine how much each outfit received when payment was made back east in Chicago. Jug glanced toward them. Eli Poole was laughing and saying something to Abe Goodrun. It didn't seem to bother Eli to be there chatting with the man he was putting horns on so regular.

A lanky crossbreed with the K5T on its hip tried to turn back from the ramp and in an instant there was a jam building. Jug grabbed the stuck animal's horn and yanked hard while he poked the steer behind it to try to back that one off. After a couple seconds the K5T got itself straightened out and went up the ramp in a rush and into the car, and the others snorted and hurried to follow lest they be left behind.

"Now, Jug."

"Keep yer britches on, Jesse." He saw that everything was moving smoothly for the moment. He threw his leg over the railing and slid down to the ground outside the chute. The air was thick with the smell of beeves and manure and filled with the sounds of clacking horn and clattering hoof and cowboy yips as the loading process went on. They had to get it done in a hurry because the train was expected along this afternoon to pick up the cars and carry the beeves off to market.

Willis Johnston climbed up to take Jug's place at the jam point on the chute. He and Jug hadn't spoken since their little incident at the Bullhorn, and Willis didn't offer to speak now either. If Willis didn't offer to, Jug wasn't going to either. Jug could be about as stubborn as anybody when he wanted to.

Jug pulled his gloves off and lifted his hat for a moment to let some fresh air reach his scalp, then replaced it, but this time tipped back just a little and not pulled down so tight. "What d' you need, Jesse?"

"We got to talk. Walk along with me." Jesse strode off down the tracks, moving along beside the empty cars waiting to be filled with cattle. With no locomotive or donkey engine to move the cars on the siding, and with the three loading chutes stationary, they had to use teams of horses to position the cars at the chute for loading, then drag them down to the west end of the siding and haul an empty one in to take its place once the first was full. The railroad crews, who knew how to handle such stuff, would couple them together again when the train arrived.

Jesse walked clean past the last cattle car and out almost to the point where the siding rails joined the main line. From here the only thing you could see to the east was bright sky, grass that was already browning despite the season, and the railroad running in an arrow-straight line into the distance with the tracks and accompanying telephone poles getting smaller and smaller to the eye. It was country that some might find empty. Jug didn't. It made him feel strong and free, not empty nor lonesome.

"Good country," Jesse observed.

"Ayuh."

"Care for a chew, Jug?"

"No thanks."

"How about a smoke then?"

"No, thank you. Jesse, you look like hell. Something's bothering you. Spit it out if there's something I can help with. If you don't want to talk, hell, we can stand here for a spell. I don't mind."

Jesse cleared his throat and spat. Stuffed his hands in his pockets. He was peering down at the ground, Jug noticed, off toward the horizon, down at the dirt again. Wasn't looking at Jug at all. Was looking at everything but.

Eventually Jesse looked up and with the air of a man delivering a death notice said, "Jug, you're being laid off."

"Laid off?"

"Goddammit, you heard me. You're fired." Jesse sounded mad as hell. That was all right. Jug understood. It wasn't him Jesse was mad at; it was the need for him to be the one delivering news like this. Eli should've had the nerve to say it himself. Instead Eli was back there having a nice chat with the man whose wife Eli was screwing. Jug didn't blame Jesse for being peeved now. Likely he was as embarrassed as he was anything else.

"Fired," Jug repeated, as if tasting the

word and letting it roll around in his mouth for a minute would let the message sink in better. "Fired."

He considered asking why. There would be a reason. The problem was that Jesse wasn't likely to know what that reason was. Lord only knew what excuse Eli told to Jesse about it. But Jug would've bet a fistful of most anything that whatever Jesse was told wasn't the real truth of the matter.

"I have . . . I have your pay, Jug. Because . . . because of your long service . . ." Jesse wasn't talking here, he was reciting lines. Somebody else's lines. Jug could guess whose easy enough. "Because of your long service to the M Bar C you'll be paid in full up to today and a month's severance pay on top o' that." Jesse dragged a hand out of his jeans and forked over a wad of folded-up canvas that looked like a piece of old wagon cover. It was wrapped into a tiny bundle and tied with string. "You can count it if you like."

"That don't matter." Jug took the packet of money and put it into his pocket un-opened.

"I don't . . ." What he "didn't," Jug knew, was know what the hell else to say. Jesse looked like he was halfway in a state of shock himself. Jug knew the feeling.

Fired. Hell, he'd been fired before. Of course he had. But it'd been a while, and that was a natural fact.

"Jug, I . . ."

"Don't fret about it, Jesse. It's all right." It wasn't all right. No way it was all right. But a man doesn't up and say such a thing.

He did have to wonder why, of course. But he'd be damned if he would go to Eli Poole and ask.

"I'll send the horse back when I figure out where I'm going."

Jesse looked startled. "Oh. The horse. It's . . . that's all right, Jug. Keep it. If you don't want to take the train out, just keep the horse. God knows you're entitled."

"Do me a favor?"

"Anything, Jug."

"Write me out a bill of sale for the horse. You can leave it at the Bullhorn. I'd give you an address to send it to, but . . ." He spread his hands and shook his head.

"I can't take it to Gerald myself. I'm going east with the cattle instead of the foreman. But I'll write it out and have one of the other fellows take it by for you. I won't forget."

Eli would be staying back and sending Jesse to oversee the M Bar C's interest in the sale. That wasn't usual. But then Abe would be going east with his cattle, no doubt. That would leave the little lady all by her lonesome back there at home. Eli would want to take advantage of that, for sure. Damn him.

"Is there anything else I can do, Jug? D' you need, like, a reference or something?"

"No, I expect folks in the basin know me good enough. If I decide t' go someplace else, well, I guess they'll take my word. Wouldn't want to work anyplace that wouldn't take a man's word anyhow."

"Sure. I . . ."

"It's all right, Jesse. Don't fret yourself." On an impulse Jug stuck his hand out. Jesse took it and they shook hands. They'd known each other . . . what? . . . fifteen years or more? As far as Jug could recall this would be the first time he'd ever shaken Jesse's hand.

But then plenty of unexpected things do happen. Shaking hands with Jesse wasn't the only one Jug could think of right now.

"You take care, Jesse."

"Yeah. You, too."

There wasn't much more that could be said and standing there feeling sorry for himself wasn't going to accomplish much. Jug went off to the bed ground to collect what little he'd brought along and saddle the horse that he hadn't expected to be needing today.

Fired. It made him feel kinda . . . empty. Like he'd lost his way in a mountain fog. Fired. Be damned!

He knelt and began rolling his bed.

24

Jug woke up. His head hurt and the taste in his mouth was positively vile. He was . . . he didn't know where he was. Someplace that . . . oh, yes. He remembered now. Sort of. He'd taken a swing east when he left Tie Siding. Instead of going straight back north to Bonner, he had gone over to Hansen's place on Muddy Branch.

Hansen's was a hog ranch situated just outside the Injun reservation boundaries. Hansen claimed it was a legitimate trading post. What it was, in fact, was a whiskey trading point. Red or white, a man could count on finding a drink there or a woman. The women were Injun and Jug supposed they were paid in whiskey rather than cash. Not that he'd ever asked — nor, for that matter, cared. What somebody else chose to do was their own affair.

He'd never had much to do with Hansen before, if only because his place was so far out of the way. Jug and some of the boys had been by there a time or two over the years, stopping off when they'd driven small herds over to the reservation for beef issue delivery — once delivered and paid for, the beeves were turned loose in a valley and the Injuns were allowed to shoot them down from horseback as if they were wild buffalo instead of regular old crossbred steers, and wasn't that a helluva sight — but none of them liked it all that much and rarely went there.

Nobody liked Hansen all that much either, never mind his place. The man smelled bad and had been wearing the same vest and moth-eaten fur hat for as long as Jug had known him. Word was that he'd been one sharp-eyed, fine-shooting professional hunter of buffalo when he was in his prime. That'd been a long while back. Now the buffalo were long gone and Hansen was a bad smelling relic who liked his own products, both liquid and fleshy, somewhat too well.

Not that it was any of Jug's nevermind.

He sat up and discovered he'd been sleeping in a pile of straw. It took him two tries to make it onto his feet. His head was spinning and his stomach felt like he'd swallowed somebody else's puke. He staggered outside the shed and got rid of everything that was in there. Didn't feel all that much better for it, but it had to be done.

If Hansen had a well, Jug couldn't see it so he walked — slow and gingerly — over to the Muddy Branch. This time of year there was enough water in it to have a discernible flow. Jug made his way a little upstream from Hansen's outhouse before he got down on hands and knees and pushed his face under until his nose touched bottom. The water felt good. Almost good enough to wake him up the rest of the way. While his head was partway underwater anyhow he took advantage of the opportunity and sucked some in, swallowing a couple quarts or so, it felt like. The water felt heavy in his otherwise empty belly, but at least it took some of the taste of old whiskey and new puke out of his mouth.

Jug straightened up and shook his head like a dog just coming out of a pond. That was a mistake. It made his head start pounding. He wiped his face with both hands then stood — on the first attempt this time — and squinted toward the sky. It was the middle of the morning. Unless it was the middle of the afternoon. He had to think for a few seconds to remember how Hansen's place was situated, then decided it was midmorning.

Of course, he wasn't for sure just what *day* this was, seeing as how he'd gone and lost track of time since he left the Siding. Didn't matter anyway. There wasn't anyplace he had to be right now nor any particular time to get there.

Jug was his own man. Free as a bird in the air. Free as . . . why the hell didn't that thought make him feel any better?

No matter.

He walked — very careful not to stagger or stumble lest someone think he was a drunk — over to Hansen's to see about having himself an eye-opener.

25

"Beer."

Hansen drew it, siphoning the brew into a tin tankard. Jug figured he knew why Hansen only used metal containers, and it had nothing to do with breakage. The man served beer that was at least half foamy head to make a barrel go further and profits all the higher.

"Five cents," the bearded former buffalo hunter said when he banged the mug down onto a plank that served as the bar here. The place must have been here a good ten or twelve years or maybe more and Hansen still hadn't built a proper bar. Not that it was any of Jug's nevermind. No, sir, it was not.

Jug dug into his pocket. Brought out some lint but nothing more.

Hansen must have seen. He pulled the mug back. Hansen didn't give credit.

"Just a minute. I got . . . someplace . . ."

He couldn't remember what he'd done with the packet of money Jesse had handed him . . . well, whenever that conversation was. "I got more."

"Take your time," Hansen offered. "I ain't going anyplace an' neither is this beer unless you come up with your nickel."

Jug encountered a lump in his back pocket. He brought it out and examined it. Sure enough, it was the folded square of canvas that contained his last pay from the M Bar C.

Jug took a stab at untying the knots in the string that held the packet shut, but the string was thin and the knots tight and Jug's fingers none too nimble right now anyhow. He abandoned the effort after only a few attempts and used his pocket knife to cut the strings instead.

He started to unfold the bit of canvas. Then froze in place as something occurred to him.

This little bundle was all prepared and ready for him.

Must have been made up before they ever left the ranch, too, because the annual spring drive to Tie Siding wasn't the sort of work that required paying boys off afterward. There weren't any saloons or whores or stores to spend money on there, for one thing. Just pens and loading chutes and the railroad tracks on an otherwise barren plain.

And unlike the fall working, when some of the hands were laid off every year in anticipation of cutting back to winter's needs, everybody turned right around and rode back to the basin once the beeves were loaded and the cars dragged away.

Paydays after the spring drive were taken care of back home and in the normal time and manner, not down at the Siding.

Which meant that Eli planned all along to fire Jug once they were away from the home place.

Hell, he'd prepared this final pay before they ever left the headquarters.

Now why ever would he do a thing like that? Jug wondered.

For that matter, why would the foreman want to get shut of a hand who'd been on the place since before Eli Poole ever came along?

It wasn't for bad work or lack of effort. Jug wasn't one to bang his own drum, but he was a solid, reliable cowhand and he damn well knew it.

Oh, there were others who could ride ranker horses and some who could throw fancier loops and maybe even some who knew cows better than Jug did. Jesse came to mind in that category. But by Godfrey there wasn't a better all-around cowboy on the place than Jug was. And there certainly wasn't anybody who knew the M Bar C range and surrounding country as well. Bar none. Jug had been riding that country right from the get-go and knew every copse, cut, cirque, or canyon where a rank beef might try to hide itself.

By dumping Jug off the payroll Poole was getting rid of an asset not a liability, if Jug did say so his own self.

So why'd the foreman plan all along to fire him once they got down to Tie Siding?

And why there instead of back in the basin where at least he'd 've had a chance to catch on with another outfit right away?

Jug had no doubt that he would find another job quick. But the decent thing would've been to let him do it back in the basin and not down here.

Not that Eli Poole was known for decency. But even so. He was a sensible foreman when it came to most things. Why not with this?

Jug stared at the bit of canvas in his hand and wondered.

"Well?" Hansen demanded.

"Well what?"

"The beer. D' you want this beer or not?"

Jug looked back down at the pay packet again. His mind was full of questions, one running after another in circles like a dog hot after its own tail. "No," he said. "I reckon I don't at that."

He turned and started out to find his gear and his horse. Behind him Hansen tipped the beer and poured it down his own hairy throat. He'd about finished it and had a mustache of white foam by the time Jug reached the door and happened to glance back.

26

It felt funny, coming back to the M Bar C like this. It wasn't coming home anymore. Familiar though it was it felt . . . strange. Different. He didn't like it. Not even a little bit.

Had to be done though. He still had gear in the bunkhouse. Lord, he'd lived there enough years. It was going to seem strange to gather it all up now and take it . . . where? He didn't know.

He rode in slowly, almost reluctantly. The outfit was already back from the Siding. Jug still didn't know exactly how long he'd been at Hansen's place, but it was long enough for the M Bar C boys to get home ahead of him. He could tell because the chuck wagon was parked inside the equipment shed and the horses from the remuda were grazing loose in the big trap. Coosie's mules were lodged in the smaller trap, and the corral behind the barn where the day's mounts were brought in to be roped and saddled was empty.

That meant the bunkhouse would be empty, too. Jug was kinda pleased that everybody would be out working in the middle of the day. He wasn't sure quite how to face all the fellows he'd been riding with now that he was laid off and no longer one of them. They would work all that out, of course. But better later on at the Bullhorn than here and now when none of them, Jug included, had had time enough to take it all in.

The foreman might've been in the big house doing whatever it was he did in there. Or he might've been off sniffing after Evie Goodrun's skirts. Jug didn't care which. He had no intention of asking Poole anything. That would only lead to Poole telling lies and the two of them having words.

Jug tied the horse — his horse now, not the outfit's — to a rail outside the bunkhouse and went inside. It was a long, dark, low-roofed structure with few windows, bunks lined up along both of the long-side walls and a slightly rank, slightly sour smell of sweat and wool, leather and saddle soap. To Jug it smelled of home, and the truth was that he regretted hell out of having to leave it.

Still, leave it he must. He went down the length of the place to the far back corner that he'd favored for so long.

The pegs over his bunk were empty. So was the striped mattress ticking that he'd filled with fresh hay not three weeks earlier while he was cooped up with that bum leg. The ticking had been emptied, folded, and placed neat as a pin at the head of the bunk, leaving the boards bare.

There wasn't a sign of any of Jug's things. Not so much as a sock tossed in the corner nor a smear of mud on the floor.

It was like he'd never lived there.

With an empty feeling in his belly, Jug left the bunkhouse and headed for Coosie's domain, which he figured was the most likely place he could find some answers. Well, short of going over and asking Eli Poole anyway.

"Foreman sent the Polack into town with your stuff," Coosie told him. "You can claim it at the Bullhorn. And he said you can't have that horse you're riding. It belongs to the outfit. Said if you came by here we're to tell you to leave it with John Weiss. Somebody will pick it up later."

"Jesse said . . ." Jug clamped his mouth shut. It didn't matter what Jesse said. And he for damn sure didn't want Coosie or anybody else to think he was whining.

"If you're hungry I can fix you up a poke to carry with you."

It was about dinnertime and common courtesy ruled that no man should ever ride away from an outfit hungry. Any guest, visitor, or passerby was always welcome to belly up to the table and help himself to whatever was there.

Except this time.

What Coosie was telling him, just as plain as if it'd been put into words, was that Jug was no longer wanted anywhere on the M Bar C. Not even for dinner.

"Keep your poke, you son of a bitch," Jug snapped. "I don't need no favors from the likes of you."

He balled his fists and kind of hoped Coosie would take serious enough offense that Jug would have an excuse to punch him. Never mind that Coosie outweighed him by eighty pounds or so and not all of it fat. It would've pleased Jug plenty to haul off and sock somebody. Most anybody.

Coosie, damn him, didn't rise to the bait. He just stood there. And how does a man argue with somebody who won't argue back?

After a minute or so, Jug gave up the challenging glare and turned around.

It was a long ride into Bonner and truth was he was already hungry as hell.

He stepped into the saddle — which *was* his, no matter what that bastard Poole might claim about the horse — and put the critter into a high lope eastward.

27

Jug turned the horse loose in the little pen behind Weiss's place and took a minute to fix his stuff up for carrying. He turned the saddle upside down and nested his bedroll and saddlebags between the skirts, then folded the cinches over them and used the latigos to strap everything down nice and tight for easy carrying. Add a nice long stick to sling it from and he could pass for a perfectly good bindle stiff. Dammit.

He was hungry when he left the M Bar C and all the more so now that dinnertime was past and suppertime upon him, so he headed first for Anna Chong's and surrounded a huge bowl of chop suey, and seconds on top of that first one. By the time he stepped out into the dark of evening he felt considerably better.

From Anna Chong's he lugged his saddle up the street to the Bullhorn. It was the middle of the week and everybody was sure to have work to catch up on at home after being away on the spring drive, so there weren't too many customers in the place. Jug considered that to be something of a shame because he was wanting to ask around and see who was looking for hands. It was a little late in the year now that the spring working was finished but, hell, there was always need for a good riding hand. Any respectable outfit would figure that, and every last one of them in the basin knew Jug and his reputation.

He ambled into the Bullhorn and dropped his gear on the floor. "H'lo, Tabe," he said to the bartender. "Is Gerald around?"

"Gone to supper. Be back later." Evans acted like he didn't want to be bothered even though the only thing he was doing when Jug came in was to straighten up the stack of glassware piled on the backbar.

"Did Siatkowski bring some of my stuff in?"

Evans just shrugged and kept fiddling with the glasses.

"Did Jesse send anything for me? An envelope or anything?"

"Ask the boss."

"Uh-huh. I don't s'pose I could get a beer."

Without comment Evans filled a mug and

set it onto the bar in front of Jug. He took Jug's nickel and dropped it into the cash box and walked away.

Tabe Evans hadn't acted like this . . . well, ever. Not ever before. He'd always been friendly enough. Pleasant. Hell, being pleasant to the customers was one of the things any bartender was supposed to do. Not this time though.

Jug was beginning to feel more than a little bit uncomfortable standing there at the bar with Evans so pointedly ignoring him so he carried his beer off into a corner and took a seat at one of the tables. Generally he liked to position himself at the bar so he could greet and visit with all the fellows who came in. Not this evening. He just plain didn't feel up to that right now, especially after the way Evans was acting.

Along about nine o'clock he decided maybe Gerald Fulbright wasn't coming back this evening. And perhaps it was only his imagination after Evans's attitude sort of spooked him, but Jug thought some of the few other customers were giving him hard looks but no conversation.

Bottom line was that the Bullhorn somehow didn't feel like the cheerful, friendly place it usually did.

Maybe things would look better to him —

to everyone — come a new day.

Jug picked up his stuff and walked out. No need to pay good money just to have a roof to sleep under, not when he'd spent half his life nearabout sleeping with stars for a ceiling. He carried his kak down to the brush that was growing along Hayden Creek and made himself a bed there.

28

"I don't understand."

"So tell me. Just what part of the word *no* d' you not understand?" Gerald Fulbright gave him a look that Jug found more than a little disturbing. It was like Gerald was looking at a cockroach found swimming in his soup bowl. "Now get your crap and get out of here. I don't want your business. Clear enough?"

Tabe Evans was standing nearby with a bung starter in his hand. The three of them, Gerald and Tabe and Jug, were naturally enough the center of attraction among the few customers who'd come in for an eye-opener.

Jug had quite frankly hoped to stretch his money by having beer for breakfast and a long visit to the free lunch spread. Now . . . now he was told he couldn't leave his saddle and stuff in the storeroom that practically every cowboy in the basin used like it was his very own closet. Couldn't put his things in there and had to take out the things Ski had brought down for him.

Jug didn't understand this. And wasn't *that* an understatement?

Still, this was Gerald's property and the man had the right to do with it — or not — whatever he damn pleased.

Jug nodded and carried his saddle outside, then came back in and got the brass bound trunk that used to sit at the foot of his bunk. He didn't look inside to see if everything was there. Wouldn't have been any point anyway. If anything was missing it would be just his tough luck. And at the moment a handful of possessions seemed mighty unimportant.

"Thank you ever so much," he said on his way out.

Once he was outside he . . . he had no idea in the world what to do next or where to head in order to do it.

Still, there was no sense in standing there like a cigar store Injun while dust settled on him. That wouldn't accomplish a whole lot.

The trunk was small but fairly heavy and for dang sure it was of an awkward size and shape for carrying, so he left it there on the boardwalk outside the Bullhorn and carried his saddle back down to the creek where he'd slept. Left the saddle there and came back for the trunk.

Once his worldly wherewithal was out of the way, if not out of the weather — which, thank goodness, had been fair of late — he walked back into town in search of breakfast.

Anna Chong's wasn't open for breakfast, more's the pity, so he had to choose between Abner Tyler's café or Manfred Haas's restaurant. The primary difference between them was the prices they charged. Although Jug had to admit that Haas did at least give diners a tablecloth to wipe their hands on in exchange for the higher cost of his meals. Jug headed for Tyler's place. It was closer.

"Haven't seen you in a while, Jug. Especially not so early as this. What can I get for you?"

"Coffee first off, Abner. And a big ol' plate of those biscuits your wife makes. I surely do like her biscuits."

"I was afraid you were gonna ask that, Jug. No biscuits today."

"She mad at you again, Abner?" Abner's scraps with his wife were legendary in the basin. No one would have cared all that much except whenever Miz Tyler — she was bound to have a first name, but Jug had never heard it spoken — got mad at Abner she sulked up and stayed upstairs in her room instead of helping Abner with the cafe. And Abner wasn't near as good a cook as his wife was.

"She is," Abner admitted. "She should be all right again after church Sunday if you want to come by again then."

"What day is this?"

"Thursday."

"I don't think I want t' wait that long for breakfast, Abner, if it's all the same to you."

"I got rolled oat porridge, Jug. Made a big pot of it this morning, and I've got Borden's and honey to pour on top."

"How much?"

"Five cents. Eight with the coffee."

"I'll take the porridge, Abner. And some coffee now if I can."

"Coming right up."

The porridge was hot and filling and even tasted good. Jug took his time with an extra cup of coffee or two while he pondered where he should go to look for work. And how he should get there. Then he laid a dime on the table next to his empty cup and bowl and went outside into the bright sunlight.

Two young hands from the XI, which most everyone except the owner insisted on calling the Eleven brand, were just coming in as Jug was leaving.

The two youngsters — Kevin and Donny their front names were — stopped square in Jug's path. Either one of them was half a head taller and about half Jug's age.

"You son of a bitch," Kevin said by way of greeting.

It probably wasn't the smartest thing Jug ever did. But he didn't really like that sort of thing for an opening comment. He reared back and hit Donny in the breadbasket just as hard as he could — figured that might take the wind out of Donny's sails for a bit, and the boy wasn't apt to be expecting it right off — then lit tooth and toenail into Kevin.

29

"Oowee!" He'd been hit harder and probably more often, too. But he sure couldn't remember just exactly when that might've been.

He struggled into a sitting position and felt his jaw. It was lumpy and swollen, but intact. He supposed that was something. He had a couple teeth loosened, but he thought they would tighten up again with time.

Had cuts over both eyes and a down-deep hurt in his belly. The good thing was that his hands stung like hell, both of them, from where he'd gotten his licks in. It hadn't all gone the way of the Elevens.

Kinda made Jug think that maybe he shouldn't go out there to look for work though. With that sort of reception the Eleven bunkhouse might not be an easy place to sleep.

He sighed, then picked himself up out of

the dirt in the alley where they'd ended up, not wanting to brawl in public.

Jug didn't consider himself to be the smartest man in the basin. But he wasn't the dumbest either and he sure couldn't figure out what this was all about. Coosie back at the M Bar C. Gerald Fulbright and Tabe Evans at the Bullhorn. Now Kevin and Donny from the Eleven outfit. Seemed like half the damn basin was pissed off at him and he had no idea why. He hadn't done anything ugly to anybody.

He hoped to hell this wasn't a general view throughout the basin. He still had money in his pocket from the severance pay he'd been given, but he wanted to find work pretty soon. Apart from everything else he just wasn't accustomed to the idea of laying around. There were plenty of fellows who liked to work from spring through the fall shipping, then lay off for the winter, go down to Denver or like that, and spend their year's pay on whiskey and whores. Jug had nothing against the idea of whiskey and whores. But he figured there ought to be more in a day than those, enjoyable though they might be in their own proper time and place. He'd always been one to prefer to work through the winter, and ever since he came to the basin he'd had enough seniority that he'd been able to choose that.

Now, having to start in with a new outfit all over again, he might not have the choice. He'd hate that. He surely would.

Nothing to be done, though, than make the best of whatever hand was dealt.

He stood, having to support himself with a hand on the side of the café building to make it upright. Somehow it seemed a long way up, and his head felt light and swimmy.

For the first time in his life, Jug felt tall. Like his head reached all the way into the clouds and his body wasn't thicker through than a hay stem.

Swayed in the wind like a hay stem, too, it did.

Swayed and . . .

Be damn. He'd gotten up, hadn't he? Stood up, didn't he?

So why the hell was he laying down now? And at that, why was he laying facedown in the damn dirt?

He was pretty sure he'd stood.

Oh, well. Must've been mistaken about that.

He tried to get up again.

The pain in his belly turned sharp and searing, shooting through his gut like a bolt of white-hot lightning.

He twisted and writhed as the fiery agony

30

"Suzy? What the hell are you doin' here?"

Her laugh sounded like a small dog barking. "And just where is it that you think you are, love?"

"In the bunkhou— Oh. No. Reckon I'm not at that." He tried to get up but Suzy held him in place with the fingertips of one hand. He was that weak. "Where am I, Suze?"

"You're in my bed." She laughed again. "It isn't like you haven't been there before, you old reprobate. But this is the first time for this reason, isn't it?"

"Have I been here long?"

She shrugged. "Most of yesterday. Or today. I'm not sure what time it is. Prob'ly somewhere in the wee hours."

"I got to get up. I got to . . ."

"What you 'got to,' Jug, is lay still. You've had the sweaty shakes so bad I changed the sheets twice already."

"But I got to . . ."

"Oh, hush up and lay still, will you?"

Jug grinned. "Maybe. If you crawl in here with me."

Suzy's roar of laughter rattled the windows and set the roof shakes to flapping. Or if it didn't it should have. "Bless your heart, Jug, you're as much man as I've ever known. And I've known some men in my time, sweetie."

"Don't I know it," he agreed with the best grin he could manage through the pain that was still threatening to cut him clean in two.

Suzy was a whore. Or had been. She was getting a mite long in the tooth for that profession nowadays. Jug suspected she wasn't but about his own age. Which in anyone's forties was bad enough. But hard as it was to cowboy with all the aches and pains, it was harder for a woman Suzy's age to bring in much of an income from her particular profession. There were younger, prettier girls available for the gents to choose from.

And Suze made it all the harder for herself by insisting that she wasn't anybody's property. She would go with a gent and turn herself inside out to earn what he paid her, but she was her own person for all of that. She didn't belong to any pimp or whore-

138

monger but went her own way.

That limited the places she could work and cut all the further into her ability to earn, but Jug had always kinda admired the old girl for sticking to her guns as — as she herself put it — an independent contractor.

There'd been a time when her stubborn streak of independence hadn't mattered. Back when she first showed up in Bonner she'd been quite a looker and of course a dozen or so years younger. She'd been a favorite of the cowboys who came to Bonner on paydays. Jug's, too.

Now . . . he guessed he hadn't been with Suzy for a year or more. Nor thought much about her. Hell, he wouldn't even have been able to swear she still lived here if anybody'd asked.

Now he was lying in her bed with what felt like rats chewing his insides and a cold sweat soaking the sheet that covered him.

"You got a good heart, Suzy."

"Shut up, Jug, and let me get some sleep."

"Sorry."

"Is there anything I can do for you, honey?" She sounded like she really meant it, too, which was another surprise.

"Yeah, Suze. Would you hold my hand?"

Her answer was a smile as she shifted her chair closer to the side of the bed and took his limp hand in both of hers.

She was still there, still holding his hand, the next time he awoke.

31

"What're you doing?" He was seated in a rocking chair in the corner with a lap robe draped over his knees and a thick shawl around his skinny shoulders. He probably looked a mess. So it was a good enough thing he couldn't see himself, and Suzy didn't seem to care. It had been . . . he had to think back . . . four days. That much he could call to mind. And the full day before that when he was unconscious. Those boys had done a better than average job on him.

Suzy looked up from her sewing. "Sewing," she said.

"I can see that plain enough, woman. I meant what is it you're making?"

"A shirtwaist for Abe Goodrun's missus." She held it up for him to see.

"Fancy," he observed.

"Do you like it?"

"Yep. It's pretty."

"Can you keep a secret?" she asked.

"Sure I can."

"I been making things, different things, for Simon Beck to sell in his store. Like this shirtwaist and some ladies' hats. Fancy braided hatbands for the gents."

"I've seen those in the display case over there. You made them?"

Suzy nodded, obviously proud of herself.

"They're nice."

"But you dasn't tell anybody, Jug. That's part of my deal with Simon. Nobody's to know where they're made or the gentle-ladies will have themselves a conniption fit and Simon wouldn't be able to sell my stuff anymore." She snorted. "You'd think a person like me was tainted or something. Lord knows I'm good enough for those women's sons, yes, and husbands, too, to wallow all over and rut on, but let me walk down a public street and the decent ladies scatter like a covey of quail and drag their kiddies along so they won't be contaminated by me walking past."

"You sound bitter."

"That's reasonable. I am bitter. Kind of. Used to it, of course. But it still makes me mad whenever I think about it." She laid the partially completed shirtwaist down and smoothed the material with gentle care. Then she turned her head to give Jug a smile and a wink. "The good thing, honey, is that I don't bother to think about it very often."

Jug rocked a little and contemplated his benefactor. Suzy was a more than commonly honest old bawd. Most her age and in her line of work would put henna on their hair or otherwise try to color it. Not Suzy. Her hair, once a gleaming and glossy black, was gray as the Old Gray Mare's and she didn't try to hide the fact.

She was tall and once upon a time she'd been slim, with handsome limbs and a shape like the proverbial hourglass. Lately it seemed some of the sand had slipped down into the bottom half of the glass and spread out there. And what remained at the top was flowing downhill, too. That which had been pert and perky was now loose and floppy, and Jug would've sworn that had gotten bigger over time, too.

She just didn't have near the enticing figure she'd come here with those years past.

For all of that though she was . . . not pretty. Even at his most lenient of moods — and considering all she was doing for him Jug had to feel mighty forgiving of fault or foible when it came to Suzy — she wasn't really that pretty anymore. Certainly not compared to how she had been. Now her cheeks sagged and there were dark circles under her eyes, and she had lines and wrinkles more than a woman her age should.

But her smile was genuine and her hands gentle, and Jug's own mother couldn't have taken any better care of him than Suzy was.

"Oh, damn!" he blurted.

"What's the matter, hon?"

"Is that rain I hear?"

"Sure. It's been raining most of the day."

He cussed a little, not under his breath either but right out loud.

"What is it, Jug?"

"Reckon my miseries are complete now. My trunk an' saddle an' things are out in the brush getting soaked."

Suzy pushed her sewing aside and stood, reaching for an oilcloth cape that hung on a peg beside the door to her one-room crib. "Tell me where it is. I'll bring it in so we can dry it off."

"You can't be going out in the rain, Suze. Cowboys do that, but not ladies."

"Good thing I ain't a lady then, isn't it? Now. Are you gonna tell me where I can find your stuff or do I have to kick through the brush along the whole of Hayden Crick until I find it?"

"I swear, Suzy, you are something else an'

144

then some."

"The longer you natter, old man, the wetter your things will be. Now tell me quick so I can get back to my work."

Jug had himself a quandary he realized and pondered upon it once Suzy was off on her errand to fetch in his gear. He owed Suze more than mere money could ever repay. If he handed over everything he had it wouldn't be enough. And come to think of it she'd never so much as hinted at wanting pay for all she was doing for him even though he was surely eating her out of house and home . . . he squinted and looked around at the Spartan quarters . . . such as house and home happened to be, that is.

There'd be time enough to worry about that when he was up and about though. He could give Suzy what he had and make some more soon as he caught on with another outfit.

Probably it wouldn't be too good an idea to go out to the Eleven brand looking for work. Considering.

But he was sure of being able to hook on with pretty much any outfit he chose. The big question now was which of the many choices in the basin would he most like to ride for.

He closed his eyes and tugged the shawl

tighter around his neck and rocked a little as he considered the question of future work.

32

There was something about the smell of saddle soap and neat's-foot oil that Jug especially liked. He didn't know why. Plenty of fellows grumbled and complained and demanded you take your gear outside whenever a body got to cleaning and oiling his tack. Not Jug. To him it was almost as nice a perfume as the fresh and yeasty smell of a clean and healthy horse, and there's not a better scent than that anywhere as far as he was concerned.

"Are you sure you don't want me to do that?" Suzy offered.

"I'm fine."

"Cleaning things, that's woman's work."

He laughed. "Not this." He'd already undone any possible damage caused by the rain of a few days back. He'd oiled and polished his saddle, headstall, bridle, quirt, boots, belt . . . even the outside of the trunk, and that wasn't leather at all but only lacquered canvas over wood.

The truth was that he was getting anxious to be on his way. He'd been lying about for over a week now and was getting antsy. Being down on his back twice in one season was just about more than he could handle. First the leg. Now this. It was too much.

"Are you hungry?"

He shook his head. By Jug's reckoning, if not necessarily that of the entire community, Suzy was a fine woman in some ways. But a cook she was not. Jug was about as good a cook as Suzy, and he couldn't hardly boil coffee without burning something.

"Do you want me to get you a bottle?"

That was one of the nice things about the old girl. She didn't have any illusions about how a man should be expected to act. He could eat beans and stay in the same room with her or take a few snorts, even scratch and spit and she wouldn't think any the less of him.

"I'm fine, thanks."

"You're fixing to leave, aren't you?" she said.

He stopped rubbing the stirrup leather that lay draped over his lap. "How'd you know that?"

"Don't you ever make the mistake of

thinking I can't read you, old man. Of course I can tell. How are you going?"

"Rent a horse, I expect."

"All right, but better you should borrow than rent one."

"It doesn't matter."

"Yes, it matters."

"It don't cost but a dollar or two to rent."

"You have to be saving your money, Jug. I keep telling you that. You don't know how long it might be before you find work again."

Jug snorted. "I don't know what you're thinking, Suze, but I'll sign on to the first outfit I show up an' talk to. Which I think will be the F R Bar. There's some pretty good ol' boys out there. I expect I could stand 'em."

"If you say so, Jug."

"Folks around here know me, Suze. They all know my work. I won't have no trouble."

"Fine, but would you do me a favor?"

"You know I will. 'Most anything you ask, Suzy. Lord knows I owe you."

"We've been through that a'ready. You don't owe me nary thing. But I would ask that favor of you."

"Name it."

"Let me give you the loan of a horse. You know. Save you the cost of renting one."

"Whatever for would you keep a horse?"

"I like to take drives, I'll have you know. I used to ride sometimes. Astride, too. Oh, that was fun. Now" — she laughed — "driving out away from town is enough for me. Will you use my horse, Jug? Please?"

"Sure, Suze. I'd be proud to."

"I don't think you should go tomorrow though. I want to take some more measurements for this shirt tomorrow. The next day maybe."

He started to say something back to her but she held the palm of her hand forward to stop the words from coming out. "Please," she said.

He knew she was concerned that he wasn't feeling up to riding again quite yet. But he was. His belly was still sore, but that would work itself out. Get him in a saddle and he'd be just fine. That was all he needed.

And he'd sure feel better when he had himself a job again. Laying out at this time of year was purely unnatural. Didn't feel right. No sir, not a bit of it.

Tomorrow . . . no, day after tomorrow . . . he'd ride out to the F R Bar and offer to hire on.

33

"I don't understand."

"What are you? Stupid? I told you twice now. The answer is no. We don't want you here. If I had ten jobs open and cattle dying for lack of care, I wouldn't want you here. Now get the hell off this place before I turn the dogs on you."

Jug couldn't believe his ears. Or rather he could believe it. He just . . . didn't understand it. He'd known Paul Darrow for eight, ten years. They'd played cards together. Drank together. Once took a very memorable beef shipping journey to Kansas City together.

Now this.

The coldness of Paul's rejection probably would have hurt like hell except Jug was too damn mad to feel hurt.

At the F R Bar, Ross the foreman had been polite in his refusal and Jug believed the man when he said he'd already hired on all the help he needed for the season.

But here at the Rocker J, Darrow hadn't bothered pouring any syrup on to sweeten the bitterness. Paul laid it on hard and straight. Just didn't say why, dammit.

Jug didn't even think about taking a wide swing past the cookhouse on his way off the Rocker J. He was hungry. It was too early to eat when he left the F R Bar and now was somewhat past noon — as the rumbling in Jug's belly kept reminding him — but he'd be double-dip damned if he would ask for a handout off Paul Darrow's lousy Rocker J after this kind of reception.

He mounted the hard-mouthed gelding Suzy had loaned him and put the horse into a lope to get the hell out of there. Paul wanted him off the place? Absolutely. Right now.

As for food, he could . . . Where could he go? He wouldn't get back to Bonner until past sundown even if he started back straightaway, and he didn't particularly want to wait that long before he put something between his belt buckle and his backbone. He'd ridden hungry many and many a time before but it wasn't a state of affairs he'd ever come to enjoy and for sure wasn't one that he liked to repeat.

"You just better think of something quick,

horse, or I'll build me a little fire an' roast your ears. You wouldn't hardly miss 'em."

The horse didn't comment, but Jug decided Suzy might not appreciate him making a meal off her animal and not offering to share.

The next best thing, he supposed, would be to swing west, over toward the Sheephorns, and show up on the doorstep of the Circle G. That would take him the opposite direction from town, but if he could get a mouthful or three that wouldn't matter. It wasn't like he had anything to get back to right off, and Suzy might like a little relief from having him underfoot all the dang time.

And while he was in the neighborhood he might just as well ask about a job, too. Abe was off east with the spring gather of beeves, but Leon would have authority to hire or fire while Goodrun was away.

"Looks like you got a reprieve, horse. Must be your lucky day." Which put the horse a leg up on him in that category, Jug thought as he reined the animal toward the distant Circle G outfit just north of his old haunts on the M Bar C.

34

Mr. Sipes — he could be called Coosie by
the hands in his own outfit, but strangers
looking for handouts would be well advised
to call him *mister* and Jug well knew it —
was decent to Jug but not overly friendly.
He grunted what Jug supposed was a greeting and without comment began gathering
leftovers from lunch and a little hot food
from the supper he'd already started cooking.

Jug sat alone at the long table in the Circle
G cookhouse and ate his fill of cold ham
and hot — if not quite yet completely
cooked — rice and cornbread with molasses poured over it. Not a bean in sight.
Maybe Mr. Sipes had something against
beans. Jug didn't ask.

"I don't s'pose the foreman's around this
afternoon," he asked when he went over to
the stove for a refill of the stout, steaming
coffee that was bitter with age. It was prob-

ably left over from breakfast. Not that Jug minded. He'd had a lot worse than this and expected he would again.

"Leon rode off someplace," Mr. Sipes allowed. "He forgot to come give me a copy of his schedule for the day."

"Pity," Jug said.

"I'll remind him this evening."

"I'm sure you will."

"You want some pie?"

"Lord, yes." Mr. Sipes had a way with pie crust. He was known for that and for his cobblers. Come the community workings spring and fall the boys all liked to slide by the Circle G wagon after supper to see if there were desserts left over.

"Over there." Sipes pointed with the tip of a heavy knife that had a blade a good foot long or more, then went back to hacking slabs of beef into small cubes. Must've been fixing to make a stew for this evening, Jug figured.

The pie was in a warming oven. There was a little less than half a pie left in one pan so Jug took that back to the table rather than dirty another dish. It was peach, made from canned peaches no doubt. Mr. Sipes had gone to the trouble of taking all the pits out. Not all cooks bothered with little details like that, but then Mr. Sipes was sure to be aware of his reputation.

Jug finished off what was left of that pie and would have asked for more except one more bite would jeopardize his belly. He was already so full he was seriously concerned about rupturing himself the next time he moved.

Still and all, he did need to move. Leon wasn't around to ask about a job, and it wouldn't have been polite to laze around on another man's place without cause. Jug figured since he was this far from town there wasn't much point in going back tonight. He'd head up into the hills and make himself a camp, then come morning he'd ride over to see if he could hire on with Bob White, who inevitably had come to be called Quail. Bob didn't have much of an outfit but he might need somebody. If that didn't work out, Jug could come back by the Circle G again tomorrow and try to catch Leon at home. At lunchtime. Jug did like Mr. Sipes's pies, yessir.

He carried his dishes over and dropped them into the bucket of soapy water put out for that purpose. "Thank you, Mr. Sipes. That was mighty fine."

Sipes grunted again and kept on slicing and whacking at the chunk of meat without looking up.

Jug belched loudly, the flavors not quite so good this time as they'd been going down, and ambled over to the cookhouse door. As he was reaching to pull it open someone shoved it from the other side and tried to walk in just as Jug was trying to walk out.

Jug found himself nose to nose with Eli Poole.

35

"I thought we'd got shut of you," Poole snarled.

He'd been drinking. Jug could smell the alcohol on his breath. And not honest whiskey either, but something vaguely sweet. Wine or brandy or something la-de-da like that.

He could also smell perfume lingering on Poole's clothing. No surprise there.

Jug was distinctly uncomfortable standing so close, his nose reaching somewhere below Poole's chin and emphasizing how much difference there was in height. Be damned if he'd back away though. Not from anything or anyone and not from Eli Poole in particular. If somebody was going to back up it would have to be Poole.

"You want some advice?" Poole said. It came out sounding like a challenge rather than a question. "Get outa this basin, mister. You aren't wanted here."

Poole wasn't the only one to express that sentiment lately, but while others saying it might hurt, Poole saying it only served to piss Jug off. He never had particularly liked Poole and the feeling was only made the worse now.

"You aren't my boss no more, remember? Keep your damn advice to yourself. Me, I'm not interested."

"You better be. I can make it even hotter for you here if you don't ride out now."

Even hotter. Jug thought Poole sounded as much like the son of a bitch was boasting as he was warning.

"Now get out of my way, old man, or I'll pound you into the ground like a tent pole."

Pound, would he? Jug'd been pounded on just about enough lately. He didn't figure to take any more of it.

Poole was bigger and younger but so the hell what?

Jug doubled up his fists and laid his best right hand onto the place where Eli Poole would've had a jaw. If he'd had a chin. Which he hardly did.

Poole should have been expecting it. Maybe he didn't. For whatever reason he didn't so much as try to duck away, and Jug's punch landed flat, as good a belt as Jug ever threw and it had every ounce of

Jug's weight and muscle behind it.

Poole's head snapped back so hard and quick his hat went sailing, and his eyes sort of rolled upward until there wasn't much but white showing.

The M Bar C foreman dropped like a slaughtered shoat. Smack down to the ground. The knees buckled and he dropped onto them. Then he gave out a little bit of a groan, almost like a sigh, and toppled forward. Probably would've landed on his face except Jug hadn't thought to step aside and so Poole fell into Jug's knees, kind of slid sideways off Jug and tumbled the rest of the way down until he was lying on his side, his front end inside the cookhouse doorway and the rest of him sprawled untidily in the dirt just outside.

"You don't seem to be much interested in advice," Mr. Sipes said from somewhere behind, "but if I was you I'd think this is a pretty good time to leave."

"Reckon I will, thanks." To get out Jug had to step over Poole, who was moaning and rocking from side to side just a little.

He walked — not in any particular hurry about it — over to where he'd left the horse, tightened his cinch, and put the animal into a slow jog out through the ranch-yard gate.

36

Jug was not in a humor for company so he rode away from town, seeking the high country where he knew the empty places better than just about anyone. No, that wasn't true. He knew this part of the country better than anyone. Bar none. There wasn't any "just about" to it.

Dusk caught him approaching the saddle that would lead — if a man knew how to avoid the blind gullies and false trails — to No Name Pass, which most didn't know so much as existed but which would take a body clean across the Sheephorns if that was what he wanted.

If a man can be said to be proud of something that was not his own creation then Jug was proud of No Name. Far as he could tell, he was the one who'd first discovered it. Well, him and some Indians, and when it came to that sort of thing everyone understood that Indians didn't count. Jug was also the one who'd named No Name. It'd seemed kinda appropriate to him, seeming a fitting moniker for a pass that wasn't supposed to be.

He had no intention of going all the way into the Sheephorns now, of course. No need for that when all he wanted was to spend a little time with nothing but stars and coyotes and the occasional elk for company.

He crossed to the north side of the saddle, ignoring what looked like an easy trail westward but was in fact just another blind lead going nowhere, and turned back east again into a small bowl filled with grass and lined with quaking aspen.

A trickle of water ran here pretty much the whole year around, and he knew he could count on finding good water this early in the season. Jug wasn't the only one that knew about the water. When he rode in, the last gray vestiges of light showed three patches of white that some squinting and close attention finally turned out to be a threesome of cow elk grazing in the little meadow.

As Jug and the horse came near, the elk drifted slowly back toward the aspen, not spooked but taking no chances. When the cows left, two dark shapes lifted out of the grass and went with them. Elk calves that'd been curled up too small to spot in the high grass until they stood and went kicking and farting to catch up with their mamas. Jug kinda hated to've disturbed them.

He dismounted not far from where the elk disappeared like wraiths into the quakies — it always amazed him how an animal that big could make itself invisible when it took a mind to — and stripped his gear off the borrowed horse. He led the animal to water, then hobbled it and turned it loose. With water right here and this stand of fine, lush grass the horse wouldn't be interested in wandering off anywhere.

He hadn't brought any food along. In truth hadn't wanted to ask Mr. Sipes for extra. But he'd eaten heavy enough at dinner back at the Circle G that he wouldn't likely starve overnight.

And he didn't have to go completely empty tonight. He put his things beside a ring of stones that he'd used a couple times before when he was up this way and blundered around in the dark fetching downed wood enough for a fire.

A little dry grass twisted into knots made jim-dandy tinder, and some twigs of aspen were plenty good for kindling. A touch of a match and he had himself the start of a fire.

Aspen isn't much for forming coals to last through the night but it makes a cheerful fire, nice and bright and crackling. It burns fast and clean, with little smoke. Not that Jug had to worry himself with smoke. There wouldn't be anybody up here and if there were they wouldn't be anybody who'd bother him. Aspen doesn't smell quite as nice as pine but then it doesn't taint meat with the smell of resin either the way pine will.

If a fella had any meat to cook, that is.

What Jug had instead of a chunk of honest beef was . . . a tin cup.

Nobody he knew went to the bother of riding around with a bulky ol' coffeepot in his gear, but a man never knows when a tin cup will come in handy. Like now.

He drank a little water cold from the creek, then refilled his cup and set it down inside the fire ring to get hot.

With a mite of time and knowledge a man could make himself all manner of teas and such from the things growing here, there, and wherever. Juniper berries . . . except of course it wasn't the season for juniper. Some mosses and lichens . . . if there was daylight to find them. Pine nuts to roast and crack and brew like coffee . . . if they were in season and the critters hadn't gotten

there first. Wild onions and camas roots and
. . . oh, and a whole heap of things.

None of which Jug happened to have
handy at the moment.

There was, however, one stalwart beverage that never failed and which, in fact,
wasn't altogether unpleasant.

Jug heated himself a cup of good old creek
water and sipped at it slow, enjoying the
warmth in his belly from the Shantytown
Tea and the heat on his cheeks and chest
from the brisk fire in front of him.

There wouldn't be anybody within ten
miles to see the light of his fire nor smell
his smoke. Up here he could relax and do
some serious thinking.

And some even more serious sleeping.

Which was what he did before he quite
got around to the thinking part of his plan
for the evening. Just kinda lay there watching a few wisps of high cloud drift along
underneath the bright sprinkle of stars and
next thing he knew he'd gone sound to
sleep.

37

"I thought we'd got shut of you."

Jug came bolt upright off his juniper bough bed, the horse blanket that was serving in place of a bedroll sliding down to his waist and letting the night air chill him. Coming summer or not, at this elevation it was still mighty cold at night.

That wasn't what interested him at the moment though.

"I thought we'd got shut of you."

He could hear the words running through his mind again, just exactly the way Eli Poole had said them.

I thought we'd got shut of you.

The son of a bitch!

This whole rotten deal was deliberate. Not just the firing. Jug'd known about that all along, of course, and in a manner of speaking didn't particularly mind it. Wrong, dumbheaded or just plain stupid, Poole was the foreman and had a right to fire him any time he took a notion.

But . . . to try to run him out of the basin?

No SOB had that right. Not Eli Poole nor a hundred others like him.

And who in hell was this "we" Poole mentioned anyway? The other cowmen? There wasn't cause for that. Jug could be accused of an awful lot of things but nothing that would get this entire basin down on him.

He tossed some sticks of dry aspen onto what little was left of his fire and saw fresh flames leap up, meaning he sure hadn't been sleeping very long or there wouldn't be anything left in the firepit but cold ash and an empty tin mug. The heat felt so good he left the blanket in his lap so the warmth could reach him through his shirt.

I thought we'd got shut of you.

The more he thought about that, the madder Jug felt.

Poole didn't just want him off the M Bar C, he wanted Jug out of the Hayden Creek basin.

Why?

Jug hadn't ever done anything to Eli Poole to make the man feel that way toward him. Not deliberate, he surely hadn't. And he couldn't think of anything he might've done accidental-like that would be all that serious either.

Hadn't ever shirked his work or laid in bed pretending to be sick when he wasn't or let any livestock be injured if there was anything Jug could've done to keep them sound. Hadn't ever pulled any practical jokes on the man even. After all, you pull pranks on fellows you *like,* not on assholes like Poole.

No sir, Jug couldn't think of one single damn thing he'd ever done to Eli Poole to make the man act like this. Him and . . . somebody. He'd definitely said *we. I thought* we'd *got shut of you.* Clear as clear could be in Jug's memory, that was. *We.* Eli Poole and somebody else. *We.*

It wasn't Jesse Canfield. Jug would've bet his bundle on that. Probably wasn't anybody else at the M Bar C either. He'd always got along fine with the rest of the boys there. Friendly, they were. All of them. It'd been a good crew and Jug had enjoyed . . . ah, hell. Best not to think stuff like that. Best to put all that maudlin crap out of mind. The M Bar C was over and done with, and Jug wasn't one for crying in his beer.

Still and all, he was pretty sure there wouldn't be anybody else at the outfit that could think up a reason to have it in for him, not even if they sat down and worked at the task deliberate.

Which meant that Poole was thinking about somebody else when he said *we*.

Some other owner or ramrod, he supposed. Not that Jug could think of any of them that might have cause. Or . . . now that made more sense to him when he thought about it.

The other part of *we* could damn well be Abe Goodrun's blushing bride, Evie. Eli was all over her like a tick on a dog's neck, and if one of them thought something the other was likely to think the same thing.

Jug grunted and considered getting up in the cold to go fetch himself another cup of water to heat for a late-night snack. Nah. He wasn't that hungry. And the air was that cold. He put the last of his wood onto the fire — he'd have to gather more if he wanted a fire in the morning — and pulled the blanket around so it draped over his shoulders like a trading post Indian, the front left wide apart to let the fire heat in.

That might be the *we* of it, Jug conceded, but it sure didn't do much toward telling him why.

If he hadn't done anything bad to Eli Poole that he could think of, he for damn sure hadn't done or said anything bad to or about Mrs. Goodrun. Hell, he hardly knew her and doubted he'd ever spoken directly to her or for that matter said very much while she was within hearing distance. Whatever he might have thought, of course, don't count.

So why . . . ?

He worried over it some, until the fire started to burn down again. Couldn't come up with anything.

He gave up for the time being and decided to sleep on it. Sometimes it seemed like he did his best thinking while he was asleep anyway.

He dragged the blanket around again so he could pull it over on top of himself and lie down again.

It was a while, though, before he was able to drop off into another sleep.

38

Well, so much for that theory. It looked like sleeping on a problem wasn't going to be good enough this time. He woke up with no solutions. What he did have when his eyes popped open was a gnawing hunger that rumbled and growled in his belly.

He'd kinda forgotten what being hungry feels like. It had been . . . what? He had to think back quite a piece . . . more than twenty years since the last time he was out of work and not knowing where that next meal was coming from. Most of that time had been right here in the basin, but he'd been employed steady before that, too.

For all those years there'd been a cook somewhere in the vicinity to serve up his grub, working out of a proper kitchen or off the tailgate of a wagon or sometimes out of a pack. But there'd never been any worries about finding a bite to eat.

And this time, of course, it was just a matter of connecting with the right outfit. He was sure of that. In the meantime he still had plenty enough money to buy his own meals.

It was just that up here there wasn't any cook to turn to nor eatery to buy from and he hadn't come away from Bonner with a poke of supplies to carry him like he would've if he had anticipated being here.

And, Lordy, he was sure enough hungry now. The late lunch Mr. Sipes gave him yesterday had been fine. But that was yesterday. This was now. And he was for dang sure hungry again.

He gathered up his things — not that there was so much to gather — and saddled Suzy's horse.

Once they got down to the flat, Bonner was still a good many hours away and Jug's gut was grumbling all the louder. The closest place where he could bum a meal would be the M Bar C but he wouldn't be caught dead asking for a handout there. The next closest, of course, was the Circle G, which wouldn't take him out of his way more than six or seven miles.

Jug wondered how Mr. Sipes was at making breakfasts.

"Whatever you'd like, just name it. I'll cook

it. You want a steak? I can cut you one. Flapjacks? Hoecake?"

"Hoecakes? Like with cornmeal and all?"

"You must be from Texas. Sure I can make you some hoecakes. Best you'll ever taste and cane sweetenin' to pour over them. How about a nice steak to go with that? You name it."

"You didn't act so accommodating yesterday," Jug ventured.

"That was before you walloped that son of a bitch Poole. Damn, it made me feel good to see him lying there puking his guts out."

Jug laughed. "He did that, did he?"

"I don't think he could get up off the ground for ten minutes after you left outa here," Sipes said, "and I enjoyed every one of those minutes, believe me."

"Not popular here, is he?"

"Not hardly. Abe is a good man. Treats everybody decent. I just wish everybody treated him as good."

"I know what you mean." Jug thought maybe the Circle G would be a good place to hire on. That would have to wait until Abe got back from selling the beeves. But it was a thought. Sounded like he'd have an ally in the Circle G cookhouse if he wanted to wait that long.

In the meantime . . . "Hoecakes sound mighty good right now, Mr. Sipes," he said. "And maybe some salt pork fried up nice an' crisp to go along with them?"

"You're a Southern boy, all right," Sipes said. "Pour yourself some coffee and have a seat. I'll have your hoecakes on the table in no time."

39

It was late afternoon and soon coming onto evening by the time Jug got back to Bonner. He could've gotten there earlier but took a little detour to see if Harold Baker needed another hand. He didn't. So Jug came back to town no better off than when he'd left.

He took the horse over to the livery, which had to be the place where Suzy kept it because the brand was the one they used there for their own stock. Willie Hilliard was there cleaning stalls and distributing fresh bedding for the night.

"I don't know where this horse goes, Willie," Jug said after he pulled his gear and stacked it beside the double-wide doors at the front.

"Just turn it in with the rest." Willie inclined his head in the general direction of the corral out back, so Jug led the horse back there, removed his bridle, and let him scamper off to drop onto his knees and then roll in the dirt like a hog in a mud wallow. Jug walked back through the barn and picked up his things.

"Whoa up," Willie said, setting his rake aside and brushing his hands on his britches as he came over beside Jug. "You been gone two full days."

"That's right. What of it?"

"She only paid for one day."

"What d' you mean 'paid?' I thought this was her horse."

"Who the hell told you a thing like that? The old bag rented this horse, and I'm telling you she only paid for one day. You owe seventy-five cents extra. Shoulda been a dollar, but he gave her a special rate. Damn if I know why. I wouldn't 've."

"You're too young to understand, Willie."

"Yeah. Whatever. Now pay me the seventy-five cents."

Jug dug in his pocket and brought out the money. He was embarrassed. Not about the fee for the hire. Hell, he didn't mind that. Nor being reminded since he didn't know about it to begin with. What embarrassed him was knowing that Suzy thought she had to give him charity like that. Jug had never looked for favors — nor taken any — from anybody his whole life long practically. Not since he was old enough to stand on his own hind legs he hadn't. Now this.

She'd meant it as a kindness though. He was sure about that, and he didn't want to embarrass her. For sure didn't want her to know that he'd paid the rest of the bill and knew about the well-intended deception. The best thing, he figured, would be to just not mention it.

Couldn't repay her for the first day's rental either, but he figured he could handle that by a side door. As a start he changed his plans about supper and went by Anna Chong's Chop House for two buckets of carryout. Anna kept a stack of spotlessly clean steel pails for folks who wanted to buy meals and take them someplace else to eat. Ten cents would get you about a quart and a half of good eating packed with rice at the bottom and the pail filled the rest of the way up with chop suey. You brought the pails back later on. Anna never collected a deposit for her buckets but Jug doubted she'd ever lost any.

The buckets were capped with heavy crockery plates tied on to keep them from spilling easy or allowing stuff to fall into the food, but that didn't prevent the aroma from sneaking out. By the time Jug got to Suzy's place his belly was growling again and he thought he could've surrounded both dinners all by himself.

"Think I'll ride out to the Lazybones today an' see do they need a hand," Jug said. To himself he made a mental note to stop by Simon Beck's store and buy himself some canned goods and stuff to keep handy so he wouldn't have to risk sleeping out with an empty belly again.

Suzy was clearing the breakfast dishes away — she'd insisted on cooking for him this morning — and Jug felt pretty good today after a sound sleep and some of Suzy's pampering. He was plenty relaxed now.

The old girl stopped in the middle of her chore and said, "I don't think you ought to do that, Jug honey."

"I got to find work, Suze. You know that."

"I know, but . . . Jug, don't go over there."

"Not today, you mean?" He misunderstood and with a bit of a leer reached after her.

Suzy turned her hips and slid away from him sort of automatically. But then she would've had plenty of practice at avoiding being grabbed when she wasn't in the mood for it. "I mean, I don't think you ought to go out looking for a job, Jug. At all."

"Jeez, Suze, a man has to work."

"I know but . . . Lord God, Jug, I hate to be the one to tell you this."

"Tell me? All right then. If you got something to say, Suzy, spit it out. I won't bite."

"It isn't me, Jug. God knows it isn't me. It's just . . ." She stopped and acted like she couldn't go on. It wasn't that she couldn't. Just that she didn't want to. After a bit her throat wobbled a couple times as she swallowed and then got a serious, determined look on her face. "Jug, there's no outfit in the basin going to hire you now."

He scowled. "Whatever the hell for?"

"It's because . . . damn it, Jug, it's because of the boys."

"What is because of which boys?" he demanded, his voice sharper than he intended.

"You know."

"No, dammit, I don't know."

"On the cow drive, Jug. It's what you done on the cow drive."

He still didn't know what in blue blazes the old bawd was talking about.

"Jug, I like you. Time was I used to have a crush on you, Jug. Did you know that? I kind of still did the other day when I found you hurt so bad. And now, I . . . I still like you, Jug. Honest, I do. As for the other, I'm not in no position to criticize other folks.

Not after all the fleshly sins I've done. I can't . . . but there's some things I never did do, Jug. I want you to know that. There was things I'd do and things I wouldn't, no matter how much I woulda been paid. I drew a line, and I never crossed over it. Still and all, it isn't my place to draw lines for anybody else. Everybody's got to do that their own selfs. You, well, I expect I was a little bit surprised when I found out how far out your line reaches. You know?"

He was still every bit as mystified as when she first brought this up.

"Sit down, Suzy. No, don't look at me like that. Sit down, please. I think you and me need to have us a talk. A real serious talk. Please." He took her by the hand — she didn't try to pull away this time — and guided her to the stool she was using for a chair now that Jug was occupying her regular chair. "Please," he said. "Tell me what you mean by all this."

40

Jug didn't know whether he ought to sit there and bawl or walk outside and hit the first son of a bitch he saw on the street. He'd never felt so awful in his life. It wasn't just the utter enormity of the lie either. What hurt him the worst was the idea that these people in the basin, these people he'd lived and worked and played among for all these years, these people could believe such a despicable and disgusting thing of him as Suzy just told him about. That they could believe him the sort of animal that would . . . he shuddered, not wanting even to think about it.

"Jug? Jug. Are you listening to me? Say something to me, Jug." Suzy's voice sounded thin and very distant. He supposed he'd been hearing it like that for some little time now. It hadn't seemed important though. Still didn't.

"Jug. Look at me."

He felt her hand on his knee and, blinking, realized she was kneeling in front of him, her face only a couple inches in front of his as she intently peered at him.

"Look at me, Jug. You're all pale, Jug. You look like a ghost. Are you all right?"

He didn't answer. Knew she was there but didn't want to bother focusing his eyes to see her better. Her features were a blur but that was all right.

"Talk to me, Jug. Are you all right?"

He closed his eyes and sighed. Suzy shook his leg back and forth in an attempt to rouse him and get him to speak. Eventually he whispered, "You b'lieved it, too."

"Oh, God. Oh, Jug. I'm sorry. You didn't . . . you didn't do none of those things, did you?"

He didn't bother answering. There would've been no point. The truth was that Suzy, apparently like most everybody else in the basin who'd heard it, believed the lie. By now that would surely include pretty nearly every man and woman in the basin and maybe some of the kids, too, although the accusation wasn't the sort of thing you would want a child to hear.

God, it was such a vile and disgusting thing.

And they believed it of him.

He'd made the lie an easy one, of course. Hell, he liked the kids who came along on those short cattle drives every year. He taught them and listened to them and advised them and joked with them.

But . . . do anything to hurt any one of them?

He felt somehow soiled just from thinking about such now that he was accused of it.

No wonder he couldn't find a job now. He was lucky he hadn't been grabbed and lynched, lucky that being pounded was the worst that'd happened to him.

And how in hell does a man prove that he hasn't done something?

It's one thing to prove an action. You can have witnesses about things seen or done. You can come up with facts and testimony and all that. It's another thing altogether trying to prove that nothing happened. What kind of witness is there to tell that something never happened?

Jesus!

He would have to leave the basin. He would have to . . .

Jug's sagging head snapped upright and he jumped to his feet, startling poor Suzy so badly that she lost her balance and toppled onto her butt on the puncheon floor of her old crib.

I thought we'd got shut of you.

Eli Poole's voice came back at him. And this time Jug understood what the son of a bitch meant. No wonder Poole thought he and this whole basin were shut of Jug's presence.

Nobody could stay with something like that hanging over him. Nobody.

I thought we'd got shut of you.

This thing wasn't just some malicious lie. It was a deliberate attempt to force Jug out of the Hayden Creek basin. Not off the M Bar C. Gone. Completely gone and out of this whole country.

Jug's misery left him even quicker than it had come over him. He could feel the hair on the back of his neck prickle. His hands bunched and extended, bunched and extended as he made fists time and again. He felt like his shoulders were becoming thicker and stronger with whatever it is in a man that comes to him when he's fixing to fight.

And this wouldn't be some barroom scrap that left the combatants friends again when it was over.

There wasn't anything uglier that anyone could do to Jug than this, and if there was one thing he was *not* going to do now it was to let himself be run meek and scared out of the basin.

No, sir. He did not think he was going to allow that to happen.

He picked up his things and walked out.

Suzy was saying something to him, yammering and tugging at him. He had no idea what she was telling him. Didn't care.

He carried his gear out and back down to the creek to where he'd made his bed that other night not so very long before.

He knew now what he was not going to do. He was not going to be run off. Eli Poole would not get shut of him that easy. Not easy and not, dammit, at all.

The thing Jug had no idea about though was what he *was* going to do about this.

41

"I'm getting the hell outa here," Jug declared. "All I want from this basin is shut of it."

"Don't think I'm gonna try to stop you," Gerald Fulbright responded. "I don't need business that bad."

"Only thing is, I don't have much of a stake to move along with. I need a horse."

"I sell beer and whiskey, not horses."

"Yes, but you and that back room of yours are as close to having a pawn shop as Bonner's got. I wanta get rid of my extra stuff. My trunk and like that."

"You'll be keeping your saddle, I expect."

"Yes, but I got some clothes. A pretty good set of Double Duck razors. The trunk itself, o' course. You can take a look."

"How about guns? You got any guns?"

Jug snorted. "Gerald, I haven't owned a gun since I was a kid. Fella called me out once in Ellsworth. He wouldn't of done that if I hadn't been carrying that damned pistol. I sold the gun that same day and haven't owned one since."

"That really happened to you?"

Jug nodded.

"What . . . I mean, how'd it come out? After he called you out, I mean?"

Jug only shrugged. Let Gerald think whatever he liked, including the assumption that Jug backed water and swallowed the insults before he went off and sold his .45 Colt. The truth was that Jug answered the challenge that day and the young cowboy died on the floor of a Kansas honky-tonk. That turned out to've been a *whole* lot worse than swallowing a stupid insult would have been. The dead boy was seventeen years old and hadn't yet shaved. Jug never felt worse about anything in his whole life than that. Well, until now, that is. Being thought evil by people he'd regarded as friends and neighbors for more than a dozen years was pretty lousy, too.

"Let me take a look," Gerald said, so Jug dragged his trunk inside and flopped it open for a stranger to paw through.

Funny thing, though. A couple weeks ago Jug thought of the Bullhorn's owner as a good friend. Now he was just another stranger in this unwelcoming town.

They negotiated a price — not a particularly good one — and Jug added that to what he had left from his M Bar C payoff.

He needed a horse, damn it, and he needed supplies to carry if he was going to ride out of Bonner.

He'd held back a few special items, knowing Fulbright wouldn't pay top dollar for them. He still had an extra nice headstall that he'd braided himself using color matched horsehair and a brush-popper's braided leather catch rope. He carried those over to Simon Beck's store.

"I can sell that bridle, Jug," Simon told him. "It's as nice a one as I've seen in a long time. Got no use for the reata though. Hell, I haven't even seen one of those short, heavy little boogers for years. Nobody up this far north knows what they are, hardly, much less would want to use one. But if you want to keep the reata I'll give you twenty-five cents for your regular hemp rope and you can carry the reata for your saddle string."

That was a better than fair offer and Jug knew it. In this wide-open country a man used a rope made out of manila, light and long and used dally style. The short, thick leather reatas used in the South were heavy enough to carry through brush where you had to be close enough to step on the heels of a steer if you expected to catch him. The leather reata had plenty of stretch in it and was used tied fast to the saddle horn. Youngsters who'd grown up working cattle in this northern country probably wouldn't have any idea about things like that. But they could nearly all make themselves whatever length rope they wanted for nothing just by cutting it off the bales of manila kept by every outfit Jug knew about. Simon buying this one off him was an act of generosity more than commerce.

Or, Jug thought, a small way of getting rid of a bad apple by helping the basin get shut of him.

When he thought about it that way he wasn't quite so appreciative of Simon's gesture.

Still, he didn't turn it down but exchanged the hemp rope on his saddle for the cherished old reata and while he was at it tied the end of the reata fast to the horn. That simple act took him back quite a few years.

The headstall and hemp he handed over to Simon along with a couple spare pocket knives he'd picked up in poker games over the years and a few other oddments of the same nature.

He wasn't rich when he walked out of the

store but at least his pockets were a little heavier than when he went in, and he figured he could afford now to shop for a horse — it didn't have to be much of a horse, just something that could carry him along slow and steady — and some eatables to tie behind the cantle with his bedroll and few remaining other things.

It was the middle of the afternoon when he was ready to ride out of Bonner.

The thing that hurt him when he did so was that there wasn't one damned soul in all the basin that he felt the need to tell good-bye.

42

He was a couple miles south of Martin Cruikshank's little farm — God knew why the man decided to farm here in cow country but everybody enjoyed the vegetables he produced, and the man seemed to be making a living at it — when dark caught him.

He would have been miles farther if he'd had a better horse. The one he ended up with was a lump of brown hair and raw bone that likely was wind-broke once upon a time. Push it too hard and it would either quit or maybe just lie down and die. It was an ugly little SOB and probably not worth the six dollars Jug paid for it.

Still, it didn't give him any trouble — probably was too weak and worn out to buck — and went in the direction he aimed it. All Jug asked of it was that it keep on doing that, and it seemed capable of handling a chore that simple.

He kept it at a slow walk and just moseyed

south following Hayden Creek in the general direction of Tie Siding until it was good and dark.

Then instead of looking for a place to sleep he reined the horse around toward the northwest. Toward the Sheephorns and the M Bar C's home range.

The way he saw this, Eli Poole was the man who'd gone and ruined him in the basin. And Eli had to have a reason for doing that. Unnecessary maliciousness is a rare commodity and not something he'd noticed in Poole before. So there had to be a reason, at least in Poole's mind.

It didn't have to be a good reason or even one that anyone else would consider to be sensible. But whatever it was, Eli Poole believed it. Had to. A man doesn't go and do something like he did without almighty serious cause.

That thought had been preying on Jug all through last night after he abandoned Suzy's place, and it was still with him.

With no way to directly find any answers — he kinda doubted that riding over and asking would accomplish much — what Jug figured to do was lie up in the hills above the M Bar C and keep an eye out for whatever happened down below. Keep an eye on Eli Poole's comings and goings in particular.

That should be easy enough, especially now that, as far as Poole and everyone else in the basin knew, Jug had pulled out.

He figured he could reach the south end of the M Bar C range even at this slow walk, stop along about first light to let the horse recuperate from the unaccustomed exercise — he had some ideas about where he could find water and grass far away from prying eyes; the final choice about it would depend on how far the horse took him by the break of day — then when the horse was up to it he could ease north again to put himself between the M Bar C and the Circle G, where Poole was certain to be going often until Abe got back.

Jug had no doubt that daytime or night he could keep out of sight once he got into the hills. He knew this ground better than anybody, and the fellows who might be looking out for the cows in the high summer grazing would be few and easily avoided.

It surely was galling, though, having to hold the dang old brown to such a snail's pace.

Jug put a clamp on his impatience and let the horse pick its way without prodding.

43

"Well, I'll be go to hell," Jug said softly under his breath. "So that's where they been going."

The horse's ears pricked and swiveled, and he had to come down off the saddle fast and jump forward to close the animal's nostrils lest it take a notion to whinny or to blow. He didn't want Poole or Evie Goodrun to hear horse noises where there wasn't supposed to be anything but elk or deer.

For the past four days he'd been watching and then following at a distance, trying to figure out where the two of them disappeared to each forenoon.

Somehow he'd gotten it in mind that it could be the two of them were up to something other than the obvious. Something that he couldn't exactly imagine but not, well, not what a man generally sneaks off with another man's wife to accomplish.

After all, Eli Poole was set on the idea of running Jug out of the basin — thought he already had done so at this point of course — and surely it had to be for a better reason than that Jug knew the man was sniffing under Evie Goodrun's skirts.

Hell, if that's all it was then he would have to chase half the population out of the basin, and Jug hadn't yet seen any sign that he had that in mind.

So somehow Jug got it in his head that Poole and Evie were up to . . . he didn't exactly know what. Working a secret mining claim on her husband's deeded land or . . . he would've believed almost anything of them. But then Jug was so distraught and distracted that it was no wonder his brain wasn't entirely in order.

What it turned out they were doing up here was . . . exactly what a body might imagine they'd sneak off and do.

Nothing more. Nothing mysterious.

They headed up into the hills each morning, rode pretty much due west from Abe's headquarters, and wound up in a small bowl on the south side of a hill Jug in his own mind always called Three Calves for the set of crossbred triplets he'd found there eight or nine years back.

The meadow was formed where a beaver

pond used to be, and a tiny creek no wider than the fingerspread of a man's one hand meandered through it. At the uphill end the flow of water trickled over a waist-high rockface and at this snowmelt time of year ran enough water to become a miniature waterfall that made music like little bitty bells dancing on the breeze.

It was a pretty place and probably a good choice for what Poole and Evie had in mind.

Jug found himself in the rather embarrassing position of being closer to the action than he wanted to be, though, when the two of them arrived in the meadow after riding there single file and acting as prim as prim could be.

Prim was not how they acted once they reached their favored spot. Evie slid down off her sidesaddle and held her arms wide as she whirled around and around so fast her skirts flew high, exposing her limbs and the downright shocking fact that Evie wasn't wearing anything underneath her riding skirt. Nothing. At all.

Jug felt his face commence to heat up, but Evie wasn't done. While Poole led the horses over to a dead tree and tied them, Evie stripped off her skirt and her blouse and her chemise until she was standing there in broad daylight wearing nothing but a hat tied under her chin and her black, lace-up shoes.

She was . . . Jug hated to admit it, but Abe Goodrun's young wife had her quite a figure. About the best Jug had seen in a good many years and for sure better than any of the working girls down in Bonner. In a way Jug almost couldn't blame Poole for being so crazy for the woman.

Not that that made it right. It wasn't. Not hardly.

And Jug sure didn't want to hang around and watch to see what all happened once Poole was done messing with the horses.

Jug couldn't quite call to mind the name they have for a man who likes to watch other folks do stuff, but whatever those fellows are, Jug wasn't one.

He backed the brown horse off nice and slow — not hard to accomplish since everything the brown did was undertaken nice and slow — and turned it around.

He was up toward the head of the bowl and for sure didn't want to go down across the open grassy meadow lest he be seen leaving, so he led the brown up higher onto Three Calves.

Just before he got to the top of the rim he heard one of the horses down below start to whicker and call. It must've taken the scent of the brown on the air spilling down into the bowl. Jug grabbed hold of the brown's muzzle again — that being the reason he was leading the horse instead of riding it — to stop it from answering and figured there was no harm done. Poole couldn't know what caused his horse to whinny. It might've been a mountain cat, a bear, 'most anything. As long as Jug's horse didn't answer it was all right.

He led the brown the rest of the way clear of the bowl and then mounted, sitting there for a few seconds to get his bearings and decide where he wanted to go next.

44

Now it is funny, Jug reflected, how a man can know this thing here and he can know that thing there, but until he puts the two of them together he doesn't always see how the one connects with the other.

It was like that once he got up onto the west side of the rim above Poole and Evie's meadow and saw the draw down below him all filled with brush and a blowdown of dead trees from a bad storm that came through long before Jug ever knew anything about this country.

He'd known about Three Calves and that tiny little bowl, of course. And he recognized the draw that lay below him now, too. It's just that for some reason he'd never approached one from the other and so hadn't ever quite realized how close together they really were.

And here he was thinking he knew this piece of country so almighty well.

Proved that a man is never too old to learn something, he supposed.

There was a trail that led through that draw that he'd followed half a dozen times or more, the last two trips — four if you count going out and coming back as separate trips through — were as recent as last year. Apart from those times he probably hadn't been up this particular trail before that since, oh, five years? Six? About that, he guessed. He could go back over it in his mind and work it out for sure if he wanted to, but he didn't care to bother.

Still, it was good to know right exactly where he was so he could go on from here.

He gave the brown its direction and let it pick its slow, ponderous, zigzag way down the hillside into the draw. Jug just leaned far back in his saddle and let his weight slide in rhythm with the brown's exaggerated hip sway as the horse carefully negotiated the steep slope.

From a distance the draw looked to be choked with brush and age-silvered tree trunks, but in truth there was a path wide and clear enough down there that Jug had guided the outfit through that way twice last year when the M Bar C delivered small herds of steers and culled heifers over to the Piegan reservation.

If there was anything they were blessed with around here it was Injun reservations. The Shoshone and Crow over to the east and the Piegan to the west across on the other side of the Sheephorns. Blackfeet and more Crow up in Montana. Sioux and God knew what else over in the Dakotas. Yeah, they had Injuns here all right and Injun reservations to keep them on. Had plenty of each.

A body would think it would make sense to put them all together in one spot so you wouldn't have to duplicate services, but no, not the fool government. Putting the Injuns all together would be logical, but the government doesn't do things in a tidy and logical manner. No, sir, not hardly.

Besides, if they tried to make the Piegan live with strangers they'd probably just fight anyhow. Seemed like all the other tribes hated the dang Piegan. But then that seemed to hold true no matter which two tribes you were talking about. For the most part one bunch just didn't seem to want anything to do with any other tribe. Jug didn't know why as they all looked and acted pretty much the same to him.

So the Piegan lived off on their own little reservation apart from the other tribes, and last year the M Bar C got an order for the delivery of two small herds to them. That was something of a first as the K5T held contracts for the beef delivery to the Injuns who lived over east and it'd been rare for anyone else to fill in. It'd happened now and then but not often.

Jug couldn't recall any outfit in the basin getting orders for deliveries to the Piegan though until those two little herds last year.

Eli Poole had been plenty happy with Jug then, by golly, for Jug's trail through the Sheephorns made it possible to take those little herds straight across instead of having to drive south to the foot of the Sheephorns, nearly as far down as the railroad, and around to the other side by that route.

Poole had been singing Jug's praises then, damn him.

And he should've, too. Jug took them through the mountains instead of around and saved weeks of travel both times — one little herd in the spring and another just like it in the fall.

There'd been seventy head delivered each time, and it hadn't even taken a lot of hands to do the job. Poole left Jesse in charge of the home place and had Jug to act as guide, plus the Polack and . . . he thought back. Billy the kid hadn't been with them for the spring drive. He hadn't been hired on yet then. But he'd been along on the fall trip.

That was the trip when Jug first really got to know the kid, and it was . . .

"Son of a *bitch!*" he yelped so loud he was afraid afterward that Poole and Evie Goodrun might have heard him clean back on the other side of the rim he'd just come over.

"Son of a bitch," he repeated in a quieter voice.

"That low and miserable son of a *bitch!*" He shouted it again. Couldn't help himself.

45

If he was right — if — it could explain a lot. If.

Seventy head of cattle trailed across the Sheephorns to the reservation last spring and seventy head again last fall. A hundred forty head driven over there last fall. A hundred forty. Same number that the winter kill report was off the mark.

One hundred forty head of M Bar C stock that were driven away in broad daylight for . . . what had it taken? . . . eight or nine days each time . . . by M Bar C hands, Jug included. But if he was right about this, Eli Poole went and stole those beeves from his employers. And while he was at it the son of a bitch stole the work of the cowboys who unknowingly helped him with his thievery.

That, Jug thought, was pretty damned low. If he was right.

He grimaced. Felt pretty sure he was right about it. The coincidence of the numbers was just too great to ignore.

Poor, stupid Eli must've been some kind of nervous once he discovered those letters all got wet and Jug put them back in order. Otherwise neither Jug nor any of the boys could've had any inkling about the theft they'd gone and committed for a foreman they trusted and against the very employer who was paying their wages.

That was disloyalty in spades, wasn't it? Like to made Jug's stomach turn.

But it fit. It was after Jug handed over those opened and sorted-out letters that Eli quit joining Jug for breakfast.

Of course he couldn't sit there at the same table. He didn't want to be questioned about things that he'd have no answers for.

Jug was willing to bet that was also just exactly when Eli started looking for ways and excuses to get Jug off the place lest he peach to the deal.

Eli needed to get rid of Jug before Jug turned around and got rid of him. SOB sure came up with a king-sized lie to get that job done, too. Jug wondered how long it'd taken him to work it out.

He could count on Jug making time for all the kids on the spring drive. He always did. Always took time for them and their sometimes silly questions. Always told the same ghost story and pretty much always taught the same few rope tricks . . . it wasn't like Jug knew so all-fired many that he could come up with new ones year after year if the truth be known.

All of that made it easy for Poole though, didn't it? Once he got the idea — and such a mean and miserable idea it was, to put something like that onto a man who'd given him nothing but loyalty — Eli only had to bide his time for a few weeks and then start the rumors to flowing.

God, it was an ugly thing he'd done.

Jug's own question now was what he could do about it.

He scowled and pondered and after a few minutes of fuming decided the first thing he needed to do was make sure he was right about this.

Then . . . well, then he'd see. He would just have to see.

"C'mon, horse. You got more walking t' do." He reined the brown higher and deeper into the Sheephorns while behind him Eli Poole and Evie Goodrun romped and played in the meadow.

46

Even without having cattle to slow things down it took the brown horse five days to cross the Sheephorns and get down into the arid sage flats to the west. Ugly damned land. Which, Jug reflected, was no doubt the reason they'd given it to the Piegan. Nobody else wanted it.

The reservation's headquarters was about as dreary as the country it controlled. Sun baked and colorless but sturdy pretty much summed it up. The few buildings were made of heavy timbers that would have been hauled in from somewhere else, there not being much in the way of trees or other greenery on the reservation land.

This was not a reservation that required the presence of troops, so the normal buildings of a military post were not needed here. The agent was a political appointee from someplace back east named Miles. He had a modest house and an administration building not much bigger.

There was a store where a licensed trader could make sure the Injuns didn't uselessly hoard any cash and a very stoutly built jail and Piegan Police headquarters, which past visits showed was used more as a clubhouse than anything remotely resembling a police station. Or a jail, for that matter.

There was also a large and largely empty storehouse where government allotments were supposed to be stored ready for delivery.

On the north side of the storehouse there was a huge and probably very expensive collection of farm equipment sitting there gathering dirt and what little rust the dry climate would permit. There were plows, harrows, mowers, and rakes by the dozen, not a single tine or disk of which had ever had the paint rubbed off with actual use.

Jug had asked about those on his first visit to the reservation. The idea, he'd been told, was to teach the Piegan to be self-sustaining. So the government bought equipment so they could farm. Didn't send anybody to teach them how to use it, but all the gear was there for them if any of the warriors wanted to take up farming.

Now where they would find water to irrigate this dry ground . . . that would've been another matter. Far as Jug knew, the government hadn't sent any dowsers to look for water.

The one building that seemed to get any serious attention was the schoolhouse, where dozens of bright-eyed and solemn kids learned English and other marvels. On his previous visits Jug noticed that the children were polite but reserved while they were in class, but once they got outside to play they were as lively and cheerful as any bunch of kids anyplace.

He tied the brown outside a stable built close to the storehouse and walked over to the agent's offices. If the presence of a visiting white man caused any commotion among the Piegan he failed to notice it. A couple dark-haired men sitting outside the police headquarters observed him but didn't interrupt the rhythm of their rocking and spitting. He assumed they were Piegans although they were dressed about like anybody he might've seen loafing around in Bonner. There wasn't a single streak of paint on their faces. It was almost disappointing.

"Mr. Miles around?" he asked the young man inside the agency office. Jug couldn't decide if the fellow was a Piegan or a Negro. It was a good thing it didn't matter because his voice didn't give him away either. His diction was as precise as a schoolmarm's and better than most preachers.

"Agency Superintendent Root is here, if that is who you mean."

"Root? What happened t' Mr. Miles?"

The clerk gave Jug a slightly haughty and definitely impatient look. "Superintendent Root's first name is Miles. Are you sufficiently well acquainted with him to address him by his first name?"

Jug shrugged. "No, I reckon I ain't."

"Would you care to see Superintendent Root?"

"Son, I've rode the better part of a week t' get here. I expect I'd like t' see the gentleman if it's all right with you."

"Very good, sir. Wait here, please."

47

Going back to the basin was not a happy homecoming. In fact, for the first time in about as long as Jug could remember, going back to the basin did not feel like a homecoming at all.

Of a sudden this was no longer home. It was only a place where there was a thing to be done, the reason being that while he knew what Eli Poole was up to and might even be able to convince others that this was so, there remained no way for him or anyone to prove that something did not happen. Whatever folks in the basin had come to believe of him through Poole's lies would remain regardless of all else, accusation being somewhat like manure on a man's britches. You can wipe at it all you want, the stain and the stink won't go completely away.

Jug knew this. He also knew the easiest thing here would be for him to keep on riding. Just quit the basin and let Poole and the others do whatever they damn pleased. He owed no man in this country. Not any more he didn't. And it wasn't any of his nevermind what the bunch of them wanted to go and do to each other.

That would be the easy and maybe the sensible way to look at it. Just go and keep going. Hook on with an outfit over east on the big grass country. Even head south, back to Texas, and see did he still have any kin living who'd put up with him when his riding days ended.

Those possibilities didn't much appeal to him although they did in truth cross his mind while he was plodding slowly along from the reservation back over the Sheephorns and into the basin by its back door.

Oh, he thought about it. Couldn't help that, he supposed.

But it wouldn't be right. If he owed Eli Poole and the folks in the Hayden Creek basin, he at least owed a sense of decency and obligation to the stockholders in the M Bar C whoever and wherever they were. He'd taken their pay for all these years. Tried to give full value for every day and every dime of it.

Thanks to Eli Poole and his stealing, Jug felt now like he was one of the ones who'd been robbed because Poole had used him and the other boys to do his crime. Jug, all of them, had gone and robbed the very ones who supported them. That was a terrible thing for a man to do, and Jug didn't like the feeling it left him with now that he knew about it.

He passed on the notion of taking the easy way without giving it consideration and turned the brown horse's nose east again.

Now that he was here in the basin again, though, he wasn't exactly sure what he ought to do next.

Confront Eli, maybe. Catch up with the man when he was in Bonner with plenty of witnesses gathered around to see and hear everything that went on and just let fly with everything Jug knew.

That might work, he thought as he sat half asleep on the back of the slow-walking horse while it followed the trail down out of the foothills.

48

Jug rode wide of both the M Bar C and the Circle G. He didn't want to take any chances of running into Eli Poole by accident. The next time they met, Jug wanted it to be at a time and place of his choosing and no other.

He approached Bonner from the south, crossing over to the east side of Hayden Creek and laying out a camp there so his few remaining things would be safe. He hobbled the horse and knuckled its poll before turning it loose. The horse seemed to like that. He was sure it wouldn't go far. And there would be no point in keeping the brown saddled and ready to run if anything went wrong when he braced Poole. A one-legged man on crutches would be able to run him down on a mount like this one.

That done he walked upstream so as to cross the footbridge into town.

Not the right thing to do, as it turned out.

He'd had it in mind to lay up in the brush, out of sight from the townspeople, until he saw Poole come in. Like practically everyone else Poole favored the Bullhorn for his relaxation, so Jug figured all he need do was keep an eye on the front of the Bullhorn. When Poole was there with a crowd around him Jug figured to sashay in and have his say.

It didn't exactly turn out like he planned.

He was half, maybe two-thirds of the way across the narrow bridge when he heard a shout from the Bonner side of the creek.

"There's the pervert, by God. *Get him!*"

It was some more of the Elevens over there. The same pair that'd been so intent on busting him up before and about three, four, no dammit five of their pals.

Jug did not mind a brawl. Hell, they could be kinda fun sometimes. But in this instance both the odds and the purpose were considerably more than he wanted to take on.

He turned and ran like a scald-ass rabbit.

49

Dammit, you'd think he was getting old or something from the way his heart was pounding and his chest aching and he hadn't run much more than a furlong or so.

Skeedaddled right past the brown horse without so much as slowing down. He could hear the young bastards back there gaining on him and if he stopped to take the hobbles off the horse and jump on they'd have him sure.

The Elevens were closer than they had been. Close enough he could hear their taunts and curses, and he didn't like the sound of them.

Any fewer and he might've fought them. Many more and that would've meant there would be some mature men in the pack and Jug figured he could finagle a chance to have his say if there was somebody willing to listen.

These young Elevens, though, they

weren't the least bit interested in talking. They wanted blood and they were wound so tight Jug was afraid they wouldn't stop with just busting him up. They acted like they wanted to carry this hate all the way to the grave.

He sprinted hard past the brown, well past the place where he'd stashed his saddle and bedroll.

Ran south until he was clear of the houses set over on the other bank of the creek and the brush grew tall and thick.

He knew he had to do something pretty quick or they'd have him because he wasn't as young as he used to be and the Elevens were gaining on him, damn their hides.

His breath felt like fire rushing in and out of his lungs, and his vision was blurring from the effort. His legs felt like they were cased in thin sheets of lead, and even his arms ached.

He stumbled as he came close to the brush. Behind him the Elevens whooped and cussed and told him what all they were going to do when they caught him.

Jug fell down. Deliberately. He could hear the Elevens yowl.

On all fours he burrowed into the underbrush, making as much noise as he could. He wanted them to be sure he was in there.

He didn't have much time to set this up though. He could hear them coming. Only a matter of rods away now and loudly sure of their prey.

"We're gonna hang you, pervert. What d' ya think about that?"

Jug made some more noise and waggled the willow stalks so they would see where he was. He laid a trail of moving willows like he was trying to double back toward Bonner, then scooted on his belly low and quiet to the edge of the creek.

Lordy, but that water was cold. It would've taken his breath away if he'd had any breath left to give.

As it was the shock of the cold water enveloping him was about enough to stop his heart. Probably a good thing his heart was racing so, he decided as he frantically searched for a stout reed.

He remembered reading way the hell back when he was a kid and attended school for those few years, remembered reading about some old time trapper — Colter, Coulter, something like that — who explored the Yellowstone country and got away from some Blackfoot Injuns by hiding out underwater. Breathed through a reed, he did. It wasn't a trick Jug ever tried. But he sure was willing. Anything to get those boys off him so he could point the finger at Eli Poole and maybe live long enough to get the hell out of the basin afterward.

He found his reed. Pulled it and like to crushed it so bad it couldn't be used. He had to slow down. Calm down. Use his pocket knife to trim the reed clean so it would hold its shape.

He could breathe through it all right. Just like that story said. Damned if it didn't work. Good thing, too. He could hear the Elevens beating through the brush upstream from him. It sounded like they weren't twenty yards off and coming closer.

There wasn't time enough to mess around. Jug shoved his head under. And realized that a person can't just lie on the bottom of a creek like a damned crawdad or something.

People float. He supposed he'd known that. Just hadn't paid it much mind. Now he dang sure did.

There wasn't any watersoaked log or anything for him to crawl under or any overhang with roots to hide behind. Just the dang creek and it not three, four feet deep along here.

He grabbed some rocks off the bottom of the creek to weight himself down. Piled what he could reach over his legs and swept some more together that he could wrap his arms around and cling to. That kept him under the water.

The reed kept him from running out of air.

But, oh Lordy, he was one cold and miserable so and so. He surely was.

50

God, he was freezing. It had been . . . what? a couple hours or so. He wasn't sure. An awful long time anyway. He hadn't heard any noises coming from above the water in ages and of course hadn't been able to see a dang thing with his eyes squinched tight shut lest he get water in them. Surely the Elevens would've gone by now, thinking he'd escaped and expanding their search farther as time went on.

That was the idea anyway.

And he had to come up pretty soon. His arms were cramping from clinging to the rocks for so long, and he'd lost feeling in most of his body. His teeth were chattering so bad he had to be careful to hold the end of the reed in his lips and suck air through his teeth.

Once he'd unintentionally bitten the tip end of the reed and closed off the air. Wriggling around trying to get it to work again he'd let the above-water end dip under for a split second and for a moment there thought he was gonna drown before he was able to swallow the water that came into his mouth and lift his head a bit so he could get another breath of air.

He had to come out. Had to. He didn't think he could stand to stay in that frigid water a minute longer.

Jug took a deep breath and then, committing himself to the surface, let the reed slide out of his mouth and carry away on the current. With no choice now but to rise he summoned his courage and what little strength he still had and let go of the rocks.

He emerged to the sound of laughter.

Oh, Lordy.

On his knees in the water with his head and shoulders above the surface he frantically wiped the water out of his eyes.

Half the damned town was standing there on the east bank of Hayden. And half of the half that wasn't on the east bank were gathered on the west bank, all of them on both sides looking like they'd come out for a community picnic or something. Some of the men had beer mugs in their hands.

"What the hell?" he demanded.

Which gave the crowd quite a laugh, damn them.

"Everybody knows that trick, for crying out loud," John Cade told him. "Besides, if you ever want to try it again you ought to keep in mind that a person can see into clear water pretty well."

"We've been watching you an' wondering how long you'd stay down," someone Jug couldn't see called out from the west bank.

"You were under more than a half hour," Simon Beck said. He looked at his watch. "The official time he broke water was four thirty-eight by my watch, and we all agreed to go by my timepiece. Four thirty-eight, boys. Who has four thirty-eight?"

They had, Jug realized, been betting on how long he would stay down.

But . . . a half hour or a little more? A half hour? Jesus! It felt like five, six times that long.

And they'd been standing up there laughing at him the whole damned time practically.

Long enough for most of the men and older boys in Bonner to join the crowd.

Which was probably a blessing of sorts, he decided, because it meant that the Elevens wouldn't have a free run to kick him to death like he'd been sure they would earlier.

But even so . . .

"Are you gonna come out now? Or do you intend to try to swim away?"

Jug tried to stand, but his legs were so cold and were cramping so bad that he couldn't. He floundered about and fell. Came up spitting and sputtering with a mouthful of creek water.

Apparently no one wanted to take the chance that he really would try to swim to freedom because several of the Elevens waded in and grabbed him none too gently by the arms to drag him out onto the bank like the biggest and sorriest damn fish ever to come out of Hayden Creek.

51

"Now looka here, dammit, I got something important t' say and . . ." That was as far as he got. One of the Elevens, one of the sons of bitches who'd beat him up the first time, coldcocked him.

Jug barely sensed the punch coming, catching only a glimpse of movement from his left. The next thing he knew there was a sound like a rotten melon being thumped, except real loud, and he was out quick as a candle flame in a windstorm.

The next thing he knew after that he was shivering cold and lying on a hard, gritty surface. The whole left side of his face felt numb and sort of lumpy. That would be from the sucker punch the Eleven gave him. Miserable SOB. Let somebody else hold him so the Eleven could hit him. Guy probably felt like a big strong man for winning that fight. Yessir.

Jug tried to open his eyes. Nothing happened. After a few seconds he realized there was nothing wrong with his eyes. For a moment there he'd thought they were swollen shut, but he hadn't been thoroughly beaten up this time. Just punched that once. He was pretty sure about that from the feeling in his face. The reason he couldn't see, he understood now, was that it was dark.

Wherever the hell he was, it was dark as a lawyer's soul. And he was alone.

That seemed sort of strange. All the menfolk in Bonner had been gathered around to capture him. Now he was alone in the dark someplace.

He moved his hands and was pleased to discover they weren't tied. Neither were his feet.

His clothes were still damp. But only damp, not soaking wet like they'd been after those hours — hour, half hour, whatever — he'd spent in the creek. He must have been lying here for a good while. Certainly long enough for it to come night. It'd been late afternoon when they got him.

Four thirty-something was the official time, for which some unsympathetic SOB won a jackpot. Thirty-eight, that's what it had been, he remembered now. Four thirty-eight. Jeez. No telling what time it was now, of course.

He lay there trying to gather both wits and strength and realized he was still so damned cold he was all atremble. Shivering and shaking like he had the ague. He'd gotten it once before. That'd been down in Mexico. This was kind of like that had been.

What he needed was a blanket or at least something dry to put over him and keep some of the cold out. He got his bearings enough to sit up and discovered he couldn't swing his feet down to the floor for the simple reason that it was the floor he was lying on. No idea whose floor, but he was on a floor. That's why the surface felt gritty. It was a floor and not a particularly clean one.

He felt around but didn't encounter anything except dirt. He wasn't sure but he thought the floor was packed dirt. Glazed with wet cow manure probably, which made for a fairly good surface, if not exactly what a man might want to fall asleep on.

He blinked and sat there for a few minutes and after a bit he thought he could make out a dark gray rectangular outline laid over the pure black of everything else. That would be starlight showing past the edges of a door, he decided.

Pretty big door, too. He must be in a shed. They'd thrown him into somebody's shed.

Oh, God, he thought.

The Elevens had yammered at him about hanging.

Please, God, they hadn't thrown him in here until daybreak so they could take him out and hang him.

He'd been shivering before from the cold. Now he had an even better reason to be trembling.

52

His clothes were dry and he was no longer so terribly cold by the time he heard them outside coming for him. They were noisy enough about it. Their voices were shrill and some of them sounded already drunk — or still drunk — even though it was early.

Once there was daylight outside he'd been able to see. It wasn't bright inside the shed but it wasn't completely dark either. Wherever he was, they must have cleaned it out to make sure he couldn't find anything to use for a tool or a weapon. The place was stripped so there was nothing left inside it but walls, floor, and ceiling. No bunk to lie on nor so much as an empty gunny sack to use for a blanket.

He'd spent the night alternately sitting and lying, leaning up against the wall opposite the doorway so if they came he would be facing them. Damned if he would present his back to them. He hadn't done anything to be ashamed of no matter what they thought.

When he heard them outside — quite a crowd of them it sounded like — he stood and brushed himself off. His face still hurt but it was a dull ache now. Apart from that, he wasn't too bad off. He did wish his boots would dry as quick as his clothes had, but the leather held the water so that his feet felt clammy and uncomfortable.

And he was hungry. Not that he expected to be served breakfast.

He heard the rattle of a chain — they'd really gone to some trouble to make sure he wouldn't get out, hadn't they? — and shortly afterward the door swung open.

The sudden rush of daylight hurt his eyes.

"You can come out any way you want. Kicking, punching, biting, if you please." Jug couldn't tell who said that but he sounded hopeful that one of those suggestions would be taken. They just wanted an excuse — some of them did anyway — to beat on him again.

Jug wouldn't give the bastards the pleasure. He held his head high and marched out into the midst of them and looked slowly around. His intention was to meet every man in this crowd eye to eye for he knew each and every one of them. Had ridden with some of them. Played with them. Drank with them.

Now . . . now Simon Beck was holding a coil of rope in his hands. New rope, it was. They hadn't yet tied it into a noose. But that was what the rope was surely for. Simon. Simon Beck. Jug had known him eight, ten years. Traded at Beck's store every month of that time, ever since he first came to Bonner. Now the man was carrying a hangman's rope.

Jug found himself wondering how it'd come to be a tradition that you hanged a man with a new rope even if it was a lynching and not a proper hanging.

It struck him that his mind was wandering off into odd places. Avoiding thinking about what was happening here, he supposed. Not that he wanted to do that. But unconsciously he was pretending that this wasn't really and truly taking place.

Except, of course, it was. Really and truly. And he damn sure better pay close attention if he wanted any hope of being able to walk away from here on his own hind legs.

"I got to tell you something, all of you," he said in a voice that was as loud and as strong as he could make it. Well, as loud anyway. He wasn't all that capable of strong just at that moment. "I got to tell you why I

231

came back here and what's behind the lies that've been told on me."

He got those words out but no more.

Saying "lies" set the Elevens off, he realized after, and they poured over him like corn syrup on a johnny-cake.

Jug got a couple decent punches in and buried the toe of his right boot in some SOB's cojones, but the odds were about twenty'leven to one and he hadn't a chance to succeed. Didn't ask for one either. He just concentrated on getting back what little he could and the hell with the rest of it.

53

He was in the shed again. Couldn't remember being thrown in, but there he was.

This time there was such a general hurting that there was no point in trying to decide what hurt the worst. Both eyes were swollen almost shut, and he could feel his shirt collar itchy and scratching on his neck from where blood dried on it and made the cloth hard. His torso and lower body felt like they were being slow roasted and whenever he tried to move the slow pains became very sharp and active ones. He concentrated on trying not to move.

He had no idea what he was doing back in here. Maybe the sons of bitches wanted to make sure he was good and awake so he could appreciate the full honor of the occasion when they hanged him. Damned considerate of them, he was sure.

They weren't taking any chances on a repeat performance out of him the next time they came for him though. This time they'd had the foresight to tie his hands behind his back so he wouldn't be able to fight back at them if they wanted some more thumping practice.

He was still able to move a little. But not much.

He made it into a sitting position on his third or fourth try and scooted back so that he could lean against the wall. The whole time he was moving he chewed on his lip to keep from crying out. Some of them might've been lurking around outside, and he didn't want to give them the satisfaction of hearing him groan, damn them.

He guessed he was in there another hour or more after he came to — no telling how long he'd been unconscious until then — before he heard a renewed commotion outside.

This time when they opened the door and a delegation of the brave ones came inside to pick him up and carry him out, hands still carefully tied, of course, he saw that they'd tied a hangman's thirteen-twist knot into that new rope Simon Beck provided.

Yessir, they were doing this right, all right.

Jug couldn't hit any of them and this time they were careful to not get in front where his boot toes could reach.

There wasn't much of anything else he could think of to express his thoughts of the moment so he turned his head around and spit in the face of the one hanging onto his right arm.

54

It wasn't too awful bad. You get to a certain point and pain doesn't hardly hurt anymore, he thought. It all becomes just a sort of overall numbness where nothing much gets through.

Which is not to say that it was fun in any way, shape, or form. But he'd 've done it again if he had the chance, damn them.

Besides, it didn't last all that long a while this time. Perhaps, he thought, this lynching business was cutting into their afternoon drinking time. And it was indeed past noon as he could see from the shadows on the Sheephorns when they finished thumping on him and lifted him — trussed hand and foot now, like a goose ready for the roasting pan — into the back of a freight wagon drawn up beneath the hayloft hoist at the front of the livery barn.

There was quite a mob gathered, drawn to the excitement as the menfolk carried him on their shoulders from one end of town clear to the other and folks streaming out to watch the proceedings, pouring out of one building after another as they marched past.

They lifted him into the wagon, and damned if Jug's old pal Eli Poole wasn't right there in the wagon bed to help steady him in an upright pose while somebody else — Jug couldn't see who but it seemed almost a shame to deny Poole the pleasure — finished messing with the rope and slipped the noose over his head.

The hemp was itchy against his flesh. All the more so after the knot was slid tight and positioned behind his left ear.

They tied the free end of the rope to a hitch ring bolted to the front of the building, pulling everything tight enough that Jug couldn't slouch without choking himself. But then, he supposed, they wanted to make sure he died with good posture.

He had to lift himself onto tiptoes so the noose didn't interfere with his throat and he could holler. "I want my last words," he roared. "I want to tell you why all this's been done t' me by my own boss, Eli Poole. I want t' tell you . . ."

Poole jabbed him in the breadbasket, driving the wind out of him and damn near hanging him right then and there when he reflexively tried to double over from the force of the blow and the loss of his wind.

"None of his lies," someone was shouting from down on the ground.

"Hang him. Hang the pervert."

"Kill him."

Friends. These people had been his friends. Until . . . what? A couple weeks ago? Little longer than that?

He couldn't breathe and his legs were losing strength so that if the mob didn't hang him soon he'd just sag lower and lower until he slowly choked himself to death that way.

"Hang him now." The voices were raw and ugly, harsh in their condemnation.

"Not yet," another voice called. That one was a woman's voice.

Jug heard the rattle and crunch of a wagon being driven and for a moment thought it was the wagon he was standing in and that the hanging had started even though he didn't feel any movement.

He opened his eyes, a little surprised to discover that he'd closed them at some point during the past few minutes although he honestly hadn't noticed that fact until now when he opened them again.

There was a buggy driving in through the crowd with the old whore Suzy handling the lines although not handling them very well. Fortunately the pair pulling the rented rig knew how to drive better than she did. Among the three of them, the two horses and Suzy, she managed to get stopped so that the side of the buggy was positioned immediately in front of the team of heavy cobs hitched to the hanging wagon.

"Not yet," Suzy repeated loud enough for everyone to hear.

Jug was surprised to see that the buggy was loaded thick with kids. The old whore was driving and all her passengers were young boys ten, twelve years old, ranging up to maybe fourteen at the most.

Behind the buggy, he saw, were a bunch more young'uns mounted on horseback, some of them riding double or even triple on an assortment of ponies and broken-down nags of the sort kids are generally given for the purpose of getting back and forth to school.

It grieved him that those children were going to see him hang. He would've rather left them with better memories of him than that.

"What the hell are you doing here?" someone demanded.

"And why'd you go and bring all these kids? This isn't fit for children to watch."

Suzy stood up and stared back at whoever it was who said that. "I got something to tell you and so do these children."

"We don't have to listen to the likes of you." That sounded like Tom Hall's voice, Jug thought, but he didn't try to see. He was having troubles enough just trying to stay standing on legs that felt like they were turning rapidly to water.

"You'll listen to me or by God I will start making the rounds of the houses in this town telling every respectable lady in the basin exactly what things their husbands like the best."

That shut them up. Jug couldn't quiet them with his appeal to speak, but Suzy damn sure shut their mouths with her threat to.

"We all know what this man is accused of," Suzy said good and loud, "but does anyone know of a single boy he's supposed to have done this to? Do you?"

She glared around the bunch of them, looking at one man and then another.

"No one wants to speak up? Well, I can tell you. You don't know of a single instance. Not one. Do you know why? Because there hasn't been any such thing happen. I know that. Do you know how I know? Because I went around and *asked,* that's how. Talk to

240

these boys. Talk to every youngster in the basin who's been on a trail drive with you grown men. Ask them. I did. Here. Tommy. You tell them what Jug did to you last year when you went with the drive."

She turned and prodded a freckle-faced boy of twelve or thirteen onto his feet. Jug remembered him. His folks lived on a hard-scrabble little outfit out east toward the Camus Mountains.

"M . . . mister Jug, he taught me how to whittle and not cut myself."

Another boy — Roy something, Jug couldn't remember his last name — stood next. "Mr. Jug taught us some rope tricks."

"Mr. Jug scared us with some stories one night."

"Mr. Jug taught me how to heel a steer."

"Mr. Jug taught me how to sharpen my knife."

The boys announced themselves one by one like it was a recitation in the classroom.

"Mr. Jug's my friend," one little guy announced proudly.

"Did Mr. Jug ever do anything, Billy, anything at all that a man shouldn't do?" Suzy prompted.

The boy gave her a puzzled look while he thought it over. Finally, very solemn, he nodded. "Yes, ma'am, he did."

Suzy blanched. It was plain she hadn't expected to hear that. But she'd started this and she seemed determined to carry it on to the end, wherever that end proved to be. "What did he do that he shouldn't have, Billy?"

"He spit in the fire close to where some beans was cooking, ma'am. My mama always gets madder'n blue blazes at my pop when he does that."

Jug heard some titters in the crowd as people tried to keep from laughing. Hell, he almost felt like it himself. Almost.

"That's the worst anyone can think of that Mr. Jug has done?" Suzy asked the boys.

She turned and glared at the crowd again, one man at a time.

Jug noticed there was scarcely anyone willing to meet her eyes this time.

And no one, none of them at all, cared to look him in the face.

It was ending. Jug could feel the shift of mood from that of a mob that wanted blood to a bunch of confused and now shamed townsfolk.

It was over, he thought. It was —

He felt the wagon lurch and heard the crack of a whip as Eli Poole jumped over the driving seat and snatched the whip out of its socket.

The big horses jumped into their harness, startled ahead and heedless of the much lighter team and buggy blocking their way. The off horse slammed into the wheeler on the buggy and drove the smaller horse to its knees.

Jug couldn't see anything more than that. The sudden motion disrupted what was left of his balance and he fell, the noose pulling tight around his throat and the hangman's rope drawing the life away from him.

55

Jug held himself rigid as a lodgepole, trying to tense his neck muscles and keep the noose from cutting deeper into his throat.

And it was working. The rope was tight, but it wasn't getting any tighter.

He held himself so tight he was practically floating. Rising right up off the ground. Going higher and high— Somebody had hold of his legs, actually. He couldn't see who. Not at first.

But somebody was holding onto his legs and lifting him up.

Somebody else cut the rope. He could feel the tension go out of it as quick as the fibers parted.

"It's just lucky you're such a little son of a bitch," the guy with his legs said.

Jug was able to look down. It was Willis Johnston, the K5T rider he'd gotten into a fight with back before things went all to hell.

"I thought you were pissed off with me,"

Jug blurted. He didn't know why that was what came out of his mouth, but it was.

"Hell no, Jug. You gave me a good fight that time. You ain't scared, man. I like that."

"Yeah, well, I expect I appreciate you pretty good right now, too, Willis."

Johnston laughed and set him down.

Somebody else — one of the Elevens — cut his hands free. "I guess . . . I guess . . ." The fellow had a sheepish, almighty ashamed look about him and didn't know how to finish. That was all right. Jug didn't want him to. About one more word and Jug would start swinging, and he was really in no damn condition for another pummeling right at this particular moment.

Willis reached for the noose, but Jug shook his head. "Let me if you don't mind." It was a pleasure he wanted for himself.

Willis seemed to understand or at any rate complied. He stepped back a bit and let Jug loosen the hangman's knot — dang things aren't as easy to undo as they are to tighten he found, but he wasn't inclined to leave the thing dangle — and drop it to the ground.

The crowd around him was quiet as a graveyard at midnight.

Jug looked around. Eli Poole seemed to've disappeared. He must have jumped down

245

off the wagon and skeedaddled. Jug could understand why.

He cleared his throat. It felt raspy and sore, but it turned out he could talk all right.

"I was wanting to say some things," he called out extra loud and the crowd, already chastened and silent, hadn't much choice but to listen to him.

"I want to tell you how this all came to be an' why. And how the M Bar C foreman has been stealing cattle from his own outfit. Every word I say you can confirm with the Injun agent Miles Root over at the Piegan reservation. That's how I know about it. I been over there and talked to Mr. Root an' he confirmed what I already suspected. Any o' you can do the same if you don't believe me."

Judging from the looks on their faces, though, this bunch wouldn't challenge him right now if he told them he'd gotten there by lifting up into the air and flying across the Sheephorns.

He went on talking. Told them about the extra drives the M Bar C made to sell beeves to the Piegans. Told them the owners back east didn't know about it. And after half a second's hesitation he told them, too, why it was that Eli Poole was wanting money so all-fired bad. After all, why should

Eli have all the fun when that faithless bitch Evie Goodrun had earned her share? It would hurt Abe to learn the truth when he got back from the east. But it would hurt him worse to spend the rest of his days not knowing what kind of woman he was married to.

Jug stood there in that wagon bed and had the satisfaction of having his entire say.

Then, empty of just about everything including pity, he crawled down out of that wagon and limped off toward where he'd left his things.

"You could change your mind, Jug. You know you could. In fact, I . . . I guess I wish you would."

Jug looked down from the back of the slow and ugly wind-broken brown horse. Suzy was by his stirrup with one hand on his knee and a pleading look in her eyes.

"I owe you, Suzy. Lord knows that I do. But I can't stay here."

She sighed. He could see that there was something more she wanted to ask.

Hell, he knew what that something would be.

She swallowed and looked about half ready to cry.

And didn't ask the question. Thank goodness. He owed her his life and it would've been hard for him to refuse her. But he couldn't take her with him. Couldn't take up with her. She was a whore, and a man just doesn't marry a whore nor let himself be kept by one. Thank goodness she knew it, too, and stopped the question before it got past the look in her eyes.

"You're a good man, Jug."

"And you're a fine woman, Suze."

"I still wish you'd stay."

"No, I've about used things up in the basin. Do me a favor?"

"Anything. You know I'd do anything for you." There it was again. But still unspoken. He could deal with it so long as she left the words unsaid.

"Tell Jesse Canfield good-bye for me when they all get back. I expect I still think of him as a friend." He leaned down and touched Suzy's cheek. "Think of you as one, too, by the way."

That was enough to start her tears flowing. "I'll tell him, Jug. I'll tell him everything that's happened."

Jug grinned. "Something else you can tell him, Suze. Let him know that if I happen across that chickenshit Eli Poole anyplace I'll sure notify the law that he's wanted back here on charges of rustling an' embezzlement." He laughed. Which was something he hadn't been sure he would ever do again just those few days ago.

"I'll tell him that, too, Jug," Suzy said. She wasn't quite able to muster up a smile. She tried, but it was no go.

"G'bye, Suze." He leaned down from his saddle and kissed her. Right on the mouth, which was something he'd never done with any whore, not his whole life long. And with the whole stinking town watching, any of them that might be interested.

The hell with them.

He straightened up and touched the brim of his hat to her, then gigged the brown lightly in the ribs and rode off toward whatever lay in front of the horse's nose.

He never looked back.

The employees of Thorndike Press hope you have enjoyed this Large Print book. All our Thorndike and Wheeler Large Print titles are designed for easy reading, and all our books are made to last. Other Thorndike Press Large Print books are available at your library, through selected bookstores, or directly from us.

For information about titles, please call:

(800) 223-1244

or visit our Web site at:

www.gale.com/thorndike
www.gale.com/wheeler

To share your comments, please write:

Publisher
Thorndike Press
295 Kennedy Memorial Drive
Waterville, ME 04901